SCOTT

CALHOUN MEN BOOK3

KATHI S. BARTON

World Castle Publishing, LLC
Pensacola, Florida
Copyright © Kathi S. Barton 2016
Paperback ISBN: 9781629895680
eBook ISBN: 9781629895697
First Edition World Castle Publishing, LLC. September 17, 2016
http://www.worldcastlepublishing.com
Licensing Notes
Cover: Karen Fuller
Editor: Maxine Bringenberg

CHAPTER 1

"I don't think I understand what you're telling me." Chloe wasn't mad, but she was pretty frustrated. This training session was taking much longer than it should have. If the man would only listen to her, she knew he'd get it. "You're saying that all I have to do is keep putting a little screw in the back of each of these here things, and that's it? All the time? That don't seem like a job at all. I think a monkey could do it."

It was on the tip of her tongue to tell him that monkeys could do it, with a great fewer questions too. But instead, she nodded at him and told him to get to work. If he did it or not, she really didn't care anymore. Today was her freedom day.

Chloe Davis had given her notice over eight weeks ago. She'd only meant to give them two weeks, but the owner of the little computer shop had begged her to stay on for another month. Well, begged wasn't really the term she might have used. He sort of tricked her into it with fat tears. So she had stayed. And then two more weeks, then two more after that. So now today was her last day. She was not going to extend her notice again. Whatever she had hoped to find there was either hidden better than her skills could ferret out or it wasn't there. She needed to move on before she made herself crazy with hunting.

She'd been working in this place since she'd left her other job, when she'd figured out they were as crooked as the people they were arresting. But it had been here. Her fellow officers hadn't bothered to hunt down here. None of them cared, it seemed, that her dad had been murdered by the people working in this little dive of a computer shop. And she was worn out. The trip, the one her and her dad had been planning when he'd been killed, was something she needed to do now so she could get a fresh start.

The trip had been something that she'd been saving for since she'd read about the cruise in the paper. Her and her dad would have four weeks of travel, a whole month for just the two of them. Sometimes in a plane, others on a ship. They were to see Europe and every other country on the list of things they wanted to do. Now he was gone and she was going to do it in his honor. And she was going to fucking enjoy it, if that was possible now.

Glancing at the clock, she was surprised to see that it was just after five. Time to leave. Chloe wasn't going to miss this place nor the people that worked here. The turnover was so huge, she'd stopped trying to make friends with the staff. Two weeks; that was about how long any of them lasted once they figured out they were working for a failing company. She was here only to find information, which she'd failed at as well.

Yesterday she'd taken all her personal things home with her. There hadn't been all that much. No pictures graced her desk like they did for the few people she worked with. There had been a little bouquet of artificial flowers, a little box that had been a birthday gift, and a blotter pad. She had pens that she'd bought over the years — most of them were cheap anyway — and a calendar.

It was old, out of date by six years. But it had special meaning to her. Her dad had given it to her, his last gift to her before he'd been murdered on the job. He'd written something for her on every day of it, even beyond the date that he'd passed away, leaving her alone in the world.

"There you are. I bet you can't wait for the weekend. Me either. To have no reason to get up until Monday morning will be a thrill." Chloe said nothing to her boss, George Flynn, as she gathered her purse and the last two things that were on her desk. "I guess you have plans for the weekend. Before coming back on Monday."

"I'm not." He asked her what she was doing then. "Oh, I'm going to sleep in. Not much however; I have things to get done all day on Saturday. But I'm not returning on Monday. I told you, several times this week, that today was my last day. I even wrote you a note, reminding you that today was it for me. I'm not coming back on Monday or any other day. I'm done."

"I can't let you go. You can't just up and leave me like this. No, no this can't be right. You said you'd give me two weeks. I need those two weeks. I've not told my dad yet that you said you might not be staying. You have to give me those two weeks. Come on, Chloe, you know that you're the only one that does anything around here. Even I don't do as much as you do." She told him that she'd given him eight weeks and she wasn't extending it again. "I can't let you go, Chloe. I really can't. This place needs you here. You're the only reason that we're still alive. My dad will be pretty upset if I let one of his best employees go without any kind of notice."

"As I've told you, several times, I've given you my notice that I'm leaving this week. Today, it's my last day. I'm done with this place." As she moved by him, he grabbed her arm. It hurt, but she looked him in the eye, and he just shook his head when she asked him to let her go. "What the hell do you think you're doing? I'm done here, George. I've worked out my notice more than I should have, and I want you to let me go."

His hand came out quickly, striking her across the face before she could think to back off. And when she hit the back of her head on the desk behind her when she fell, Chloe felt sick to her stomach, the pain was so bad. But she was more upset that he'd hit her for leaving when it was scheduled.

George pulled her back up, never loosening his grip on her arm. "Look what you made me do, Chloe. And I can't let you go. I never told anyone that you gave your notice, so see, it's fine. You can come back on Monday and no one has to know that you were leaving. You can't anyway. I want you to stay here. My dad will too. Once he finds out that you're carrying this company all on your own. He said that we have to stay in business. That it's imperative that we never close our doors for any reason. So he'll be thrilled to know that, you know, I was able to make you stay. And I'm going to. I need you to stay here. I can't keep this place open without you being here."

She jerked from him and felt her skin burn in pain. Something was wrong with him, she thought. And he was dangerous too. Chloe had noticed over the last several weeks that he'd been coming into working later and later and then leaving early. And he was acting strangely. She was pretty sure that he was stoned about all the time now; she'd seen enough of it on the job to know what it looked like.

"You'll have to learn to live with disappointment. I certainly have. Now, I gave you my notice and I'm leaving." Standing up, she made her way to the door, afraid now for the first time since she started working here. She spoke to George over her shoulder, keeping her distance from him in the event he tried to hit her again. "I have held up my end of the bargain and I'm leaving here. Today."

Going down the elevator to the lower level, she held onto her things like a lifeline. This place had gotten stranger and stranger, and she was glad to be quit of them. But as soon as the doors opened, she knew she was fucked. Security was there when she got out of the doors.

Chloe wasn't sure what they thought they were going to do, but she tried to hand the first one her badge and he wouldn't take it. This was surreal. She was leaving and they were barring her from it. It wasn't like she was running off; she'd given her notice. She wanted to scream at them.

Taking out her phone, only meaning to take their pictures, she flinched when the man to her left knocked it out of her hand and crushed it under his boot. Chloe was terrified now and wasn't sure what she was going to do. Normally she was armed, as she had a concealed weapon permit, but she'd left it at home today. Then the door behind the security team opened and a tall elderly man came in and looked at her. For some reason she thought that this man alone could take all the security team alone, but she also didn't want him to get hurt.

He was holding one of their bags, a large one that had the name of the company, Flynn Ark Computers, blazed on the side. She'd bet anything he was bringing it back because it no longer worked. Which was, sadly, par for the course of this place.

He looked at her, then at the men, and asked her if she

was all right. One of the security team drew out his gun and had it pointed down at his side. This shit was getting too real. But she was desperate and needed to leave.

"No, they won't let me leave. They're detaining me from going home for the day. I hate to say this, but I need your help. George Flynn, the man behind me, has already hurt me by slapping me. Please, can you help me?" The elderly man just stared at her, then he moved away.

She just knew that no one was going to help her, and she wasn't even sure what was going on. Then the elderly man came back, his arms now free of the computer bag he'd had in his hand. He stood there, his arms across his chest as he sort of rocked back on his feet.

"I haven't a clue what the devil is going on here, but that little lady there said you hurt her. Is that right? 'Cause I'm thinking she wants to leave here." George started talking behind her. How he needed her to stay. "I don't care a little bit that you want her to stay. The thing is, she don't want to. And in my book, that trumps what you want. You and your men, you back on up now, and me and her will get ourselves out of here."

"You can't just come in here and take one of my employees. I tried to explain to her that she can't go, and she just won't listen. Now you just go on and toddle away and we'll get this fixed. She'll want to stay here when I explain it to her." The elderly man only cocked a brow at George. "She needs to work here. I want her to. I don't know why she'd even want to leave here in the first place. Just because I let her give me that paper saying she was leaving doesn't mean that I have to let her go. This might be a crappy job, but my dad said I have to keep the doors open, and if she's not here taking up my slack, then we'll be out of business."

He wiped at his nose, something that he'd done several times while standing there. When he came away with blood on his hand, he pulled out a hand towel and wiped it away. The strip of cloth was nearly covered with blood, both fresh and dried. The elderly man snorted and then laughed.

"Well, sir, she don't seem to think so, and if she wants to go then I think you'd better let her. In fact, I'm gonna have to insist on it. You just don't treat women the way you are. They're too precious for that to be going on." He told her to come to him and she did, as far as she could before the armed guard stopped her. "You just back off, boy, and we'll just be going about our business."

"Look here, old man, I don't think you heard me well. I told her that I'd let her go when I had enough people that knew her job. Nobody knows her job as well as she does. And it's hard to replace her. Not that I tried all that much, but she can't just leave me in a lurch like this. My dad will be pissed." The nice gentleman told her again to come along with him and they worked their way to the door. "You're not leaving here, Chloe. I told you, you're going to work for me. And you damned well will until I say differently. I'm in enough trouble with my daddy as it is."

Rocket, one of the security team, stepped in front of them when they were right in front of the door. The low growl coming from the older man startled her, but she held on tight to his hand when he took hers. The man was going to get hurt because of her, and she was worried about that. When Rocket backed away, his head down, Chloe thought they'd be free when two more men came at them. They were going to die, she thought. Just because she'd given her notice like a good employee. The elderly man laughed a little and she looked at him.

11

"You see them men out there?" She looked outside of the building through the big glass door and nodded. "You go on out there with them and when you're safe, I'm gonna kick me some bottom in here as soon as I get me some reinforcements." She looked at the nice man and put her hand on his shoulder. He wasn't going to get killed because of her, damn it.

"Just come out with me. Those men, they look like they could keep us safe. Come out with me." He just gave her a little shove and she ran into something hard. She looked up into the face of one of the men that had been standing outside. "They're going to hurt him. Please, make him come out with me."

"Grandda?" The elderly man said he had this. "Maybe so, but she's afraid, and if you get your ass handed to you, I'm going to have to kill these men. And then Grandma is going to eat you and us alive for letting you get hurt. Don't you think this would go a lot better if you just come with us? I do."

"She's always been a party pooper, your grandma. You know that, don't you? But they were about to kidnap this here girl. She asked me for help. Not you and them others, but me. And I'm just chivalrous enough to want to help her. This here man, he's trying to say she is gonna do something she don't wanna. That ain't right in any book and you know it." He turned from George to look at the man that held her gently by her arms. "You thinking I can't handle these young men here? You might be right. I don't think they're gonna play fairly anyways. That's why I asked you to come on in and help me out."

George tried to take her from the man holding her. He didn't get the chance before the man behind her not only growled like the other had, but grabbed George's hand and twisted it. George went to the floor like he'd been tossed there, and didn't look like he was going to be getting up any time soon. She hated to be glad at someone else's pain, but he'd slapped her first, and she had a feeling that he'd have done a lot worse had these men not come to help. George started shouting almost the moment he touched the floor.

"You mother fucker. I don't know what's going on here or why you resorted to violence against me, and frankly, I don't really care. But she isn't leaving. I told her, over and over, that I need her here. Chloe is the only one that does her job and does it well. If I let her leave, then my dad is going to be very upset with me. She has to understand that I cannot be in any more trouble with him. He'll cut me off, and I need that money." George cried out when the man jerked his wrist again. "That fucking hurt, you bastard. Come on, Chloe. You just go back and retract your notice and then I'll see you on Monday, just like normal. Then we'll talk about how you're going to make it up to me for this man hurting me. If you don't, then I'm not sure what's going to happen to your last check. You know that I can hold it."

"Chloe, is it?" She nodded at the man behind her. "My name is Trent Calhoun. That's my grandda, Trent Calhoun the third; he goes by James. Those other men, the ones out there waiting on us, are my brothers. Not that you need to know who they are right this moment, but you can trust them. And if you'd be so kind as to go out to them, I'd really appreciate it. Grandda and I have to talk to these men about respecting other people's wishes."

"They'll hurt you." Trent stretched his neck and she heard it pop. Looking at George now, she shook her head. No, she thought, they'd hurt George, and right now, she didn't care as much as she might have at one time. "These men will hurt you, I think. And after this, I really could care less if they did.

13

I'm not sure where all this came from, but I wouldn't work here now if you gave me a million dollars. You're a prick."

She heard the older man, James, laugh, and she turned to the door again. The guards there didn't look like they were going to move, but she saw the door open and two of the men from outside were there with her. The guards, seemingly as a single unit, moved back out of their way. While not outnumbered or outgunned, they were certainly out smarted and out muscled. The Calhoun brothers were frigging huge in comparison, and she thought more dangerous even unarmed. Chloe looked back at George and his men. Turning when one of the brothers said her name, she looked into his eyes that seemed bright with humor.

"He wants you to come with us." Chloe had no idea why but she was willing to go with these men, anywhere so long as it wasn't here. Not just because George was being so weird and scary, but she had a feeling that they'd not harm her. Moving out onto the sidewalk, she let out a breath that she'd been holding. The younger of the two men spoke again. "Are you all right? Did he hurt you?"

Nodding then shaking her head, Chloe frowned when the man laughed. Pulling her sweater sleeve above her wrist, she showed him her arm. The bruise there was huge already, and a perfect imprint of a hand. It sort of made her sick to her stomach to know that someone would hurt her like this over a job. When the police showed up, she looked up at the man who had asked after her injuries.

"They had to be called in. He was trying to detain you. And while you did get away, we have to cover our own butts so as not to get sued for helping you. Besides, I'm pretty sure that my grandda was going to hurt one of them. He cannot stand the unjust, as he calls it." She thanked him and he smiled at her. "You're not going to like the fact that you're going to have to go to the hospital, are you?"

"I'm fine." He shook his head. "No, really, I've been bruised before. This is no big deal. I just don't understand what came over him. For the last few weeks, he's been…well, he's been off his rocker, I guess."

"I'd say that you've got that about right. But you're going to be safe now, so don't worry too much over it. But I have to insist that you head on over to the emergency room. That way you have a record of what was done to you and why we had to step in." She tried to tell him she was fine. "Fine or not, you need to have someone look at that. What if it's sprained really badly?"

In the end not only did she end up at the hospital, but the men, all four of them, stayed with her. She hadn't felt this protected since her daddy had died. George had sprained her arm. The bruising would go away and she'd heal, but she just didn't understand what had come over him.

~~~

James sat in the lobby and watched the comings and goings of the people. There were all manner of sickness and hurts coming in. The nurses and staff were doing their best, but there just weren't enough of them to go around. When the seat next to him moved, he looked over at Scott.

"They send you here to bust me up too?" Scott told him it was called busting his chops, but no, he'd just come by. "That man, he was hurting that girl. Scared her some too, I think. He just wasn't gonna let her go without a fight."

"Trent said that he was high. No excuse, mind you, but that can affect a person's thinking. Also, I had Joe make a few calls. Flynn's dad is on the way to the station to see his son. I guess William Flynn, his father, is on some of the boards that you're on around town. Flynn the senior has been putting his son in some rehab places for a few years now, and it's never taken. Or whatever they call it. Joe said she'd let us know what goes on down there. In addition, and this is just my opinion, I think there is more to this than him wanting her to retract her notice. Trent said he was rabid about it almost. Do you know William?" James nodded and looked at his grandson. "I'm fine, Grandda. I promise you."

Yesterday when they'd been working in the shop, Scott had just dropped to the floor. James had never been so terrified in his entire life. And when Scott finally came around, he'd made him sit on the floor for another hour before he'd let him stand. James thought for sure he'd lost his grandson.

"You been to see that quack?" Scott told him he had an appointment tomorrow. "You should go on up to that desk and tell them what you told me. That ain't right and you know it."

"I'm just exhausted. I've not been eating as well as I should; the house is coming along nicely now and I've been putting in too many hours. I really need to hire me a cook and someone to clean up after me all the time." It didn't make him feel any better about his grandson, but James thought that might help some. "Grandda, I promise you, I'm just tired."

"Why? What are you not telling me? Something happening you don't want to share with me? Hell boy, I done told you everything about me." Scott said he knew, too much. "Well, I want you to know me inside and out. Now that we're going to live forever."

"You still pissed about that? What are you going to think when those great grandbabies come along? That you sure wish you didn't have immortality?" James glared at Scott. "Don't give me that shit. You know as well as I do that you're

16

going to be walking that little girl down the aisle and acting as if you invented living forever."

"Ever tell you that I don't like you much?" Scott laughed and James felt it all the way to his heart. "You gonna find you a mate and forget about your old grandda. That's what's got me so tied up."

"You know better than that. You are my world. And any woman that comes into my life is going to have to know that." Scott looked around the lobby of the hospital much like James had. "They're understaffed here. Trent said he was going to try and get some of the younger pack to go to college to be nurses and doctors. Not only that, but whatever they want to do. We have set up different scholarships for them. He's also setting up a clinic for the pack."

"I heard tell that man that's coming in with his new business, he's moving here too. That'll sure help with the money flow around here. He's been buying up a few of the properties about and helping turn them into shops and such. I heard tell that he's having some issues out there in the building department. You know anything about that?" Scott nodded and told him it was permit issues, but he thought Joe was handling that. "I sure hope so. He's gonna bring this town back to its former self if he keeps that up. I guess the land out there, it's been cleared of everything, and they've started on the construction of his plant."

"The men and women working on the construction are applying to work in the plant once it's up and running. At first it won't be as many jobs as we need, but Doug said that within a year he'll have over a thousand jobs to fill here. And I guess Joe is working on another guy to come out and put a plant in." James was right proud of his grandchildren. And loved the women that they'd been mated to as much as if they

17

were his own. "Grandda, is that the doctor?"

They both stood up when a man in a white lab coat came toward them. Trent had gone home, telling them that he'd see them later. Both Sterl and Elijah had left as well, telling him that they'd be around should he need them. James had been dealing with pricks like the one in that place even before these kids had been born. And now they were treating him like he was some kid. He was a grown man, damn it.

"Miss Davis is getting dressed now. She has a sprained wrist that we've wrapped up. And there is some tearing to her skin that I'm not worried about, but it is painful to her. The bruising will fade after some time, but she'll need to be watched for a while, I think. She's a little shaken up by this." James said he'd be too if a man he worked for hurt him. "Yes, about that. Mr. Flynn has called here and said we were to detain her. I guess he's thinking that somehow what happened is all her fault. This is with the backing of his security team too, I guess. Whatever that little shit told his daddy, he is bringing the police. If I were you, I'd not wait around for them."

"Damn it all to hell and back. When?" The doc said they had about twenty minutes. "Well, that rules out walking out, trying to get her going all gentle like. They'll be coming with their lights and sirens running for sure now. You willing to help us spring her?"

"Yes. I have also taken pictures of her injuries, had her write out her statement with a witness, and have given her copies of everything." James and Scott made their way to the curtained area as the doctor continued. "She's aware of the police coming and why. I also suggested to her that she needs to leave with the two of you. Her home will be watched as well, so they'll head there next if I don't miss my bet. I don't know what sort of burr he has up his butt about her, but I don't think I'd wait around to find out."

Scott said he'd get the car. James wasn't sure what he was gonna do with a pretty little thing, but he'd sure keep her safe. Nobody should be afraid to leave their job, not like she'd been. Chloe came around the curtain just as he was reaching for it. She looked so upset that he felt his wolf run along his skin needing to protect her.

"I don't know what to do. I didn't do anything and now the police are coming. And I know them well enough to know that they're going to hurt me worse than George did. What the hell is going on around here when a person can't just quit their job without pain and suffering?" Grandda told her he didn't know and that he had it. "Yes, I'm sure you do, Mr. Calhoun, but this man is after me. And while I'm afraid, there isn't any reason for you to be involved any more. I can handle him."

"They're coming here to arrest you, or worse, like you said. That boy of his, he sure enough told a tale that will get you into trouble, if I don't know any better. And when they do get here, there might be a lot more bloodshed than they think if they try and take you against your will...or mine, for that matter. Men like William Flynn, they get what they want simply because they think they can. I don't cotton to that, no ma'am, I do not." James knew William well enough to know that he was a bastard and a bad man to do business with. And to his way of thinking, the apple never fell far from the tree. "You come on with us and we'll put you up proper like. Then when we figure out what the heck is going on with them, we'll help you get yourself settled again. All right?"

"I don't know why he's doing this to me. I gave him my notice, and even worked past it to help out. But I have plans. Damn it, I never did a thing wrong while I was there. I even, against my better judgment, tried to help him out by trying to train a few of the people I worked with on how to keep the place running." He gave her a gentle nudge toward the front of the lobby and she went with him. "What is wrong with people nowadays? My dad would have kicked his ass for treating an employee like that."

"Your daddy need to be called?" Chloe told him he'd been murdered. "I'm sorry, darling, I am. But we're going to have to get our feet moving here."

He saw them before they saw him and Chloe. James pushed her into a curtained area and told her to be still. As the police moved by him, he reached for Scott and told him there was a change of plans, and to meet them at the back entrance. Pulling Chloe along when the police moved down the hall, they nearly ran out of the department.

By the time they were nearly out of the hospital, his heart was going a mile a minute. He wasn't worried about the police or the other men, but he was excited. He'd not had this much fun in years. Well, not all of it was fun, but he was enjoying himself a bit too much. He wasn't worried about the girl getting hurt, but he was worried about the police. They could be a little off at times. Jasmine touched his mind just as Scott was pulling the truck up in front of them.

You old poop, what are you doing now? He told her as he opened the door to leave the hospital. *Trent said that that man hurt that girl. Is she all right? You bring her here. I'll help you take care of her.*

She's not a puppy, Jas. She's a full grown woman. He laughed because he'd been thinking the same thing. *I'm gonna bring her there. She's got nowhere else to go for now. That dumb butt done went and called the police on her.* He told her he'd be there soon, that Scott was there with the truck now.

James got in once the girl was in the back seat. He looked over at Scott when he'd not moved. Saying his name got him nothing, so he snapped his fingers in front of his face. Scott looked at him with the most pained look, and James felt his fear for his grandson double.

"Son?" He shook his head. "Come on now, what is it? You hurting? Scott? Tell me. What is it?"

"Nothing." He started the truck but James put his hand over his before he was able to shift. "Grandda, this is neither the time nor the place for this. The police are coming now. And...and I'd appreciate it if you'd just leave it alone for a moment."

"Hell no, I'm not going to do any such thing. You tell me what ails you or we're going to sit right here until them police come out here and arrest us all." Scott looked at him again and James felt a moment of fear. Scott's wolf was moving along his skin like he was ready to do some terrible business. "Scott?"

"She's my mate." James was so shocked by the confession that he leaned back in the seat and looked at them both. The girl was his mate? That pretty little thing was Scott's mate? As they drove out of the parking lot and onto the road, he started laughing. That, of course, pissed off his grandson.

"You gotta admit, this is just perfect." Scott asked him why. "Well, she needs some protecting, and there ain't no better man in the world for the job than you. Might even shake your world up a little."

"Excuse me, what are you talking about?" James looked at Chloe and thought of her as his granddaughter. "I'm not sure what you think is going on here, but I'm not a mate to anyone. Not now. Not ever. I have plans."

"Yeah, well, so did I, but I guess neither of us is getting

21

what we want." James started to tell Scott he was going to get more, so much more, when he turned to him. "Don't. I don't want to hear about how my life is better now. How I'm going to be the happiest man in the world. I'm not, so let it go."

James held his tongue, the hardest thing he'd ever done. He reached out to his Jas and told her what was going on and what Scott had said. James glanced back at Chloe and noticed she was just as hard set on this not working as Scott, and told his own mate.

I'd not worry about it, James. They'll work it out. He told her that the girl had already been hurt once today. *And I'm sure she will be again before this is done. Bring her here like you wanted and we'll sort this out.*

He wasn't so sure that there would be any sorting today. And he doubted very much if Chloe was going to be staying with them. Scott might not be happy about having a mate, but James knew he'd care for her with his life.

CHAPTER 2

Scott kept an eye on Chloe the entire drive to his grandparents' home. He wasn't sure what he was supposed to do with her. Not that she was an object that he had to put on a shelf or something like that, but he didn't want to take her home with him. Well, that wasn't true either.

His house wasn't like other homes...not like those of any of his brothers or his parents or grandparents anyway. He'd been working up until a few weeks ago, and now he had the stuff from his clinic in his house. And it was set up. Stretching his neck again, he wasn't really surprised to hear from Trent.

So, you want to talk about this? He asked him what he meant. *You having a mate. Not being really thrilled about it. That the police are after the three of you. Any and all if you want to.*

No, I don't want to talk to you about having a mate, nor how thrilled I am about it. The police, that has nothing to do with me so I have no answer for that. Who told you, anyway? He told him Mom had. *Figures. Grandda didn't waste any time, did he?*

I think he's worried about you. He said that you're not happy about this. Scott asked him why he should be. *Because she's your mate, your other half.*

So? That is no more a reason than that idiot at the shop she was just at gave her for staying. Trent, I'm not really the mating kind of guy. I'm more of a…I don't know, more of a love them and leave them sort of guy. I have sex with whips and belts. I like it rough and painful. When Trent said nothing, Scott continued. *My idea of taking a woman is to tie her to a cross and beat her ass until she's screaming in pain. Then for fun, I might fuck her until she's ready to come but don't let her. That's my idea of fun.*

Some of what he said was true, but not all. He would never hurt her that way. Yes, he'd have sex with her the way he liked, but he'd give her pleasure too. And never in a way that she wouldn't enjoy too.

Are you finished? I mean, do you feel like you shocked me enough? Or would you like to add how you use gag balls and pearl beads? Scott felt his face heat up, forgetting that Joe might have talked to his brother about some of the shipments that she'd help him put away. *She's your mate. Do you suppose that she might enjoy a good bout of your kind of sex too? I mean, it's not like you're an asshole or anything. Just a man with different ideas about it.*

No one likes sex like I do. Which wasn't true, and he was sure that Trent knew it. *I'm what most would consider a deviant.*

Yeah, while there are men and women out there doing things to their partners pretty much like you do, but don't give a shit if they're enjoying it or not. Nor, for that matter, if they live when they're finished. At least you're open about your sex life. He was too, maybe too open. *Where is she now?*

He looked at her in the rearview mirror and saw a tear roll down her cheek just before she wiped it away. Scott wondered if she was hurting still, and thought perhaps he'd been the one to upset her. Telling Trent where they were, he parked in front of Grandda's house.

Whatever you decide, your house or leaving her there, let me know. This Flynn character is out for blood, I think, and he's going to come after her. Why? I have no idea, but they've got the police out in force looking. Scott asked Trent why this was such a big deal to them. *I really don't know. She gave her notice, worked it out and then some, and now they're going after her. If the police were given a reason for this, I've not heard. Joe is looking, but for now, we're just working to keep her safe.*

As soon as they all three got out of the truck, he followed her to the porch. Scott didn't touch her, no matter how much he wanted to, but he did watch her. She was upset, and he thought that it was more than just being his mate that was doing it. When Grandma came out on the porch with them, she hugged him and Grandda, then looked over at Chloe.

"That man, George Flynn, he's a little bastard." Chloe nodded and smiled. "You come on in the house and let me have a look at you. I'm to understand that you've an idea that we're not human."

"No, ma'am. I mean yes, ma'am." Chloe looked at him before continuing. "Yes, ma'am, I know that you're more than likely not human. He thought I was his mate. But I don't know what you are."

"Wolf. And I didn't say I thought you were my mate; I said you were." He watched the anger just wash over her. It was beautiful, and he was pretty sure that she was holding a good deal of it down inside of her. Like she was bottling up whatever had happened to her recently. Scott wasn't sure why, but he thought that she needed to let it out. "And when I get you to my house, I'm going to show you just what I expect you to be doing for me as my mate."

The punch to his face was unexpected but well deserved.

When she came at him again, this time with both of her hands doubled up, he grabbed her body and turned her so that her back was to his chest and her arms were crossed over her. He held her this way until she calmed a little. His grandma left them there with a short nod, taking Grandda with her.

As Chloe was still struggling against him, he let her to a point. Scott knew that if he let her go she'd hurt him, so he just held on. He wasn't stupid enough to think she'd not hurt him again if given a chance. But he knew that something was hurting her beyond today's events. When she finally settled down, he continued to hold her just for the simple reason that he liked having her close to him.

"Are you all right now? I think you needed this. To vent some of your anger. I'll let you go if you promise not to hit me again." He watched her struggle again. "Take whatever anger you have at what was done to you out on me, and then we'll talk."

"You're hurting me." He didn't think he was but he did let her go. When she turned to him, he could see tears in her eyes. "I don't know what I did to make him do that to me. I worked really hard at that job. And I even gave notice and helped them out when it was obvious they needed someone to replace me. George didn't do anything, not a thing to find someone to take over my responsibilities. And the few that he did hire, they weren't fit to work there. Nor did they last that long. It was as if he didn't want anyone to come in. I had to get out of there. I have plans, I want to go on a trip. I've earned it."

"Yes you have. And I don't know what he was thinking either. My brother said he was high. And that whatever story he told his dad has him coming after you." She nodded as if she figured as much. "Did I really hurt you?"

When she lifted up her arm again, he felt horrible. Scott took her in the house and yelled for his grandma. As soon as she joined them, Grandma started fussing with her, taking her to the kitchen to get her cleaned up. The blood on the bandage had his wolf snarling at him as he made his way to follow the two of them. But Grandda stopped him before he could.

"Do you know who she is?" He shook his head. "I think I might have known her daddy. Mike Davis. You remember the name?"

"No I don't." Then it hit him. "The cop. The one that was killed a few years back. He was helping...I don't remember who, but he was helping someone on the side of the road when a car hit him and dragged him several hundred feet before he was dropped. Christ, she's his daughter?"

"I'd say so. Mike was a good guy, one of the best. His death is still unsolved so far as I know." Scott remembered the day it had happened. He'd been on his way home from a conference and had read about it in the papers. "You hurt her just now. Wanna tell me why?"

"She needed to vent, just as I told her. I think she's bottled it up inside." Grandda asked him if he'd seen this before. "Yes. I have."

He didn't tell his Grandda that he'd been there too. Was there now. He needed to let off some steam himself, get out and hit someone or something, but he couldn't, not without consequences. His wolf wasn't calm like his brothers'.

"I want you to do me a big favor. I want you to try your best to go slow at this." Scott asked his grandda why. "Don't know. But like you said, I think she might be holding onto something deep. Maybe her dad? I don't know that either. Could be this Flynn person. But whatever it is, I'm thinking she's got to be taken into this family a little slower than most would."

"You think she'll run?" Grandda said he didn't know that either.

As they made their way to the kitchen, he could hear his grandma fussing over Chloe. As soon as they entered the big room, Scott felt his wolf run along his skin.

"What was that?" He looked at Chloe, not sure what she was asking him. "That…I don't know. Like this really strange tightening around me. I think it was coming from you."

"My wolf." He wasn't sure what to think when she told him she'd felt his wolf. There were times when Trent could feel him, but usually he was able to control that. "I'd like to fix your arm since I hurt you."

"How would you do that? And why?" Instead of answering her, he lifted her arm up and licked along the tears in her skin. "Christ."

Scott looked at her and felt his wolf again. As he stared at her, licking over the last, smaller wounds, he could hear her pulse rate pick up, her blood flowing faster through her veins. He was having a hard time holding his beast in, and when she put her free hand on his cheek, Scott felt him calm down.

"He's very strong." Scott told her he was. "I knew a wolf once. He and I would hook up to go to dinner together sometimes. Company things for him when he needed someone on his arm. Things like that. But his wolf, he was calm in comparison to yours, I think."

"Mine is different than those even of my family." She nodded and looked over at his grandma. Scott did as well. When she smiled at them both, Scott had a feeling that she was thinking this mating thing was a done deal. But it was far from that. He looked back at Chloe. "My home is not far from here. I think, for the time being, you'd be safer there than here.

And while I'm doing some renovations, you can tell me what you want."

"I don't want anything. And why would you even think I would? I told you, this is not going to happen. I have things I want to do, and being nursemaid to an over grown shifter isn't going to be a blip on my list." Before he could answer her, she spoke again. "This is just a small misunderstanding between George and me. And as soon as I explain what is going on, I'm sure that they'll just back off. I know that he's doing drugs, but once he figures out that I'm leaving and not returning, I'm sure that he'll apologize."

"There is an arrest warrant out for you." She looked over at his grandda. "Heard about it just a bit ago. Joe, my granddaughter-in-law, she's got herself some insider information, and she said that George has been bailed out and that he's pressed charges against you. Not sure what for just yet, but we're working on that. Basically, he's claiming that you're the bad guy in all this and he wants you arrested. I'm assuming, and I could be wrong, that he's going to drop the charges as soon as you come back to work for him. That part, I just don't understand. Why would he go to this extreme if it was only to have you working there?"

"This is insane." Scott had to agree on that. She'd been the injured party in this, not George. "I'm not going to be arrested. I didn't do a damned thing wrong, only try to leave. You were there, you saw him."

"I did. I did. But that don't make a never mind to those people down there at the station. When people start throwing their weight around and greasing them up some nasty palms, things get done that shouldn't be." Grandda looked at Scott. "You two stay for dinner and then we'll work on it from there. I'm thinking that no matter what we do, they're not going to be happy to find her here."

"Why not?" When Grandda didn't answer, he looked over at his grandma. "What's going on? Why would they be less happy to find Chloe here?"

"Because, my dear boy, they know that you do not mess with the Calhoun's. And I believe that your grandda has had dealings with them before. None of them good ones." Scott asked her when, but this time, he got no answer. "Grandma? What's going on here?"

"I bought the darn building he's got his computer place in. William has been paying me rent now, and has been way behind for a while. Not that I needed the money or nothing like that, but he was really ticked off that the bank sold it to me. He kept telling me it was a mistake and that I'd robbed him. Then a few months ago, he contacts my attorney and tells him he wants to buy it. No matter the price. Well, I told him that I don't have a price because I don't want to sell. And that made him a little mad." Grandma snorted. "Okay, he's a lot mad. Telling me that he's gonna buy it no matter what. Then he started on this campaign to make me sell it to him. Sending me letters and whatnot. He even tried to get the bank to close up my accounts. Stupid wiener head."

"How the hell did he think that was going to work? I'm assuming that the bank laughed at him and told him that wasn't going to happen." Grandda told Chloe that they had at that. "Then why would he threaten someone when he couldn't afford it? And why does he want it so badly? I mean, sheesh, there has to be better buildings in the area. No offense, but that one is sort of out of date and needs a major overhaul if you ask me. Why doesn't he just move to one of the other buildings that he can buy? Seriously, it's not like there aren't several close to him that are empty. Why not buy one of those and get the hell out of that building?"

"You'd think that, wouldn't you? But he's got a burr up his bottom now and he's not taking no for an answer. Maybe, and I don't know for sure, but maybe he knows where you are and has it in his head that this'll bring me around." Chloe told him not to do it, she'd done nothing wrong. "No, you've not, darlin' but that don't mean that he's gonna give it up. He's about ten times a fool for thinking he can outwit me."

Scott had to agree with them both, it was about the dumbest thing he'd ever heard. He had sold his own building just last week, getting a nice profit from it to boot. He had yet to tell his family, but he'd purchased two more buildings in the depressed area just to hang onto them. Scott wasn't sure what he'd do with them, but for now he owned them.

Dinner was take out. He and Grandda went into town and picked up both Chinese and some pizza. Grandma didn't care for the first, and loved pizza more than he did crab Rangoon. It was a fun meal with great people, and he learned a great deal about his mate too.

She was indeed Mike Davis's daughter, and was still hurt that his murderer had gone unfound. Chloe had an apartment that she hated, but couldn't stand the thought of living in her old home where her dad had lived. She also had a car that ran only when it felt like it, even though, according to her, she could afford better. And she had a degree in business management, as well as criminal law. He found out, just from the conversations around the table, that she'd been a cop at the station house until about a year after her father had been killed. Also, and this one made his wolf hum, she wasn't afraid to stand up to him.

"I'm not a pushover." He told her he could see that. "And I don't appreciate you trying to make me do something that

31

you want. I can take care of myself, and have been for quite some time. I'm not going to go to jail, and I'm certainly not going to be your mate. I want you to get that notion right out of your head."

Before he could point out to her the illogic of all her statements, the doorbell rang. His grandparents were still in the kitchen, having run him and Chloe off to the living room while they dealt with the cleanup, so he went to the peep hole to see who it might be. Three officers, the Flynns, as well as their attorney were standing on the front porch. Scott told her to go to the kitchen. Of course, she refused.

"They're not going to be nice about this." She told him that she wasn't either. "All right, but if it gets nasty, so will I."

"Of course you will. You're a man." While he wasn't sure what she meant by that, he opened the door anyway. As soon as guns were drawn, he let his wolf take him.

CHAPTER 3

Chloe kept glancing at the large wolf that was standing next to her. She was terrified that he was going to leap out the door and kill the men standing there. Holding onto his fur seemed futile in that she knew it wasn't going to hold him back if he wanted to jump, but she had to do something or blood was going to be shed.

"Miss Davis, if you could please have Scott go in the other room, I'm sure we can talk about this." She only stared at the officer. She thought his name badge said Holden, but she wasn't sure, because not only was it on upside down but it was covered up as well. "We only wanted to talk to you."

"And that's why you drew your weapons on me? To talk? Do you even know the rules of engagement, you moron? What did you suppose I was going to say to you that shooting me was going to be an option? I'm not even armed at the moment." He didn't say anything but hadn't put his gun away either. "I asked you a fucking question, and I demand an answer."

"We heard how you beat Mr. Flynn here up, and we weren't taking any chances." She looked at George, who was

33

a good head taller than her and outweighed her by at least a hundred pounds. "Size doesn't matter."

"All men say that. Next you'll be telling me that it's all in the performance." Joe, who had shown up about five minutes after the cops had, laughed, and so did Scott's grandda. "You come to these peoples' house, guns drawn and in force like I'm going to take you apart. You are only supposed to draw your weapons if you feel threatened or if I have a weapon myself. Scott was a person until you idiots drew your guns like we were lined up at a firing squad. So unless you anticipated that he was going to shift, which was a reaction to your actions, then bravo to you for being a clairvoyant. But, and this is just me, if I were you, I'd be more concerned what might happen to you if I were to release this wolf here. I'm well aware that he might not be able to outrun a bullet, but you might miss and I know he won't. I'm willing to guarantee that some of you are going to die. Are you willing to take that chance?"

"Are you threatening these men?" She looked over at the elder Flynn when he spoke, and wondered if he realized that pushing away from the table sooner might save his life. The man had to weigh at least four hundred pounds, and more than likely it was more than that. "You hurt my boy here, left your position before your notice was up, and now you're here threatening the lives of these fine officers? My goodness, you sure do have a filled up dance card. Why don't you just come along nicely and we'll get this taken care of. You should know that hanging with these people will only make things worse for you."

"If we were dancing, you fool, then I'd not be standing here holding back a large wolf." When Scott lunged at the men, she nearly laughed when William screamed like a little girl. When he sat back down on her feet, she wasn't sure if he was telling her he had her back or he was keeping himself from leaping again. "I gave my notice over two months ago. If you don't believe me then I can have a copy of it sent to you. Also, not only was it emailed to him, but it was sent by certified letter that was signed for by George. After giving my notice, the day I was to leave, George begged me to stick around until he got someone trained to take my place. He admitted to me today, in front of witnesses, that he'd not even tried to find someone. And that you'd be pissed at him again for not making me stay. Did you teach him to manhandle women who didn't do what he said?"

"Sometimes women, such as yourself, need to learn who the bigger fish is. And it doesn't mean a damned thing, you telling me that you sent him a letter. For all I know, you could have sent him a love letter. Is that it, he spurned you and now you're taking out some sort of revenge on him?" Scott growled and she felt it all over her body. "You let him go and there will be hell to pay, young lady. I'll have these men shoot him and you if you get in the way."

"Will you now? You'd better be worried about me, you arrogant fucktard. I'm way scarier than he is." She wasn't sure where all this bravery was coming from, but she was pretty sure he was going to call her bluff. "What the fuck are you doing here anyway? I'm reasonably sure you weren't invited."

"You hurt my son." She looked over at George, who was grinning at her. It was then that she noticed that he had a little dust on his upper lip. And his nose was bleeding. When William turned to see what she was looking at, she knew that he'd seen it too. "Will you fucking clean up? Do you have any idea what an embarrassment you are to me? You had one fucking job, one, and you couldn't even make that work."

"Dad?" When the elder Flynn wiped his own nose, George

35

did the same. "I have a cold. And that's my meds. But I did tell her she had to stay there, that you'd be pissed off at me again. And I was right. You are."

Without a word about his lie about the cold and the meds, William turned to her. He hated her. She could see it right there on his face. When James moved to stand on the other side of her, it occurred to her that it was the elderly Calhoun that he was looking at and not her.

"William, got yourself a stellar kid there. Upstanding and all. I'm surprised that he's not running for some sort of office, the way he throws his weight around and bullies one of his own employees. And between the two of you, you sure do have some considerable weight, don't you? I told you when you gave him that shop that it weren't gonna do you no good. The kid ain't got a lick of sense in his fool head." James laughed then. "In the event you don't get it, I'm being sarcastic. I don't do it as well as some, so I thought I'd explain myself."

"Like you have children that are any better than mine? Christ. That boy of yours, what's his name? TJ something or another. Anyway, have you seen the way he runs around town with that younger woman? And what do you think people are saying about that?" William laughed, and so did James. Chloe had no idea who the other man was, nor the younger woman, until James spoke again.

"That's a right fine father-in-law I have in a son, if you ask me. Taking his newest family member to the doctor and making sure that she's all right. Well, in my book that's the way it should be, don't you think?" The officer to William's right leaned in and whispered. "You might want to listen to your boy there, William. You don't have anything on this here girl and you know it. And if you're thinking of making up something that we both know didn't happen, then you can go ahead and try that angle if you want. But I got news for you…I'm a betting man, and I'd bet you don't have a toe to stand on."

"I tell you what, James. You sign that building over to me and we'll just make this all go away. I'm willing to bet you don't need that building for anything anyway." William glanced at her before continuing with James. "Your kids, they don't need to be worrying about this stuff after you're gone. And you know as well as I you're pushing your time here on this earth."

"You think so? Well, I just might want to live forever. Yes, sir. I think I will. Just live forever. And while I'm at it, I might just watch you and that boy of yours rot away in prison."

"What do you think you know?" Chloe heard the panic in his voice, the way his eyes darted around like he was afraid. "You don't know shit, James, and we both know it."

But she did. It was why she'd taken the job there in the first place. To see just how involved, if at all, George had been in the death of her dad. And she'd come to the conclusion that not only was he involved in it, but that his daddy might know about it too. But wherever the evidence was, it wasn't in the big falling down business. At least not where she could find it.

Scott yawned and laid down on her feet. Chloe wasn't sure if he was holding her there or he was just resting. But she had a feeling that he was doing the first. She was about ready to slam the door in the face of these idiots anyway, and be done with the lot of them.

You do that and you'll only make them madder. She looked down at Scott when he spoke to her. *Yes, I can speak to you, and you to me should you want. When I sealed up your wounds, I made a connection with you. Just think of me and then talk in your head. Sort of like a thought. I'll get it.*

37

Nice trick. But what do you suppose is going to happen if they get me to go with them? Not that I want to, but they do have a gun. He told her to wait, the wagons had begun to circle around them. *What the hell is that supposed to mean?*

Before he answered her, even if he was going to, she heard the crunch of gravel in the driveway and looked out beyond the men. In that moment Chloe wished that she had a camera. No one would believe her when she told them about the men who had gotten out of the two trucks behind the cruisers.

Almost as if they sensed they were no longer alone, William and the cops turned. The cops backed up and pulled their weapons up to aim them at the newcomers. But in seconds, less she thought, not only were they tossed to the porch but their weapons were gone as well. Vampire, her mind screamed at her, and she tried to take a step back.

His name is Noah. And he's a friend of the family. He won't harm you. She wasn't so sure. *I promise you, he'll never harm you.*

I've been told that before. Vampires aren't the friendliest of people even on a good day. Scott promised her again that she'd be safe. *We'll see.*

"Hello, William. George. How's things going? I heard from my dad that you're here making a nuisance of yourself." She watched this man too…Trent, she remembered his name from the office today. There was an air about him that screamed for you to give him the respect that he deserved. It could have also been the fact that he had five full grown men behind him that looked like they could have been his clone. "I've brought my brothers around too. You know, to watch you get your ass handed to you. Dad is here as well. We're just one big fucking happy family."

"William. Acting like a fool again are you? Why don't you gather up your minions and give it a rest? I'd really hate to see one of these fine boys of mine mess up their night by having to tear your throat out." TJ, the father of the "boys" behind him, stretched his neck, much like Trent had done earlier. "I'm not in the mood to mess with the two of you. Get in your cars and leave here now."

"TJ, this is no concern of yours. I'm here to have this woman arrested. She assaulted my son and caused him bodily harm. You and your boys go on about your business and I'll attend to mine." TJ walked up on the porch with the rest of them, his sons right behind him. "TJ, this has nothing to do with you or your family."

"The minute you came up to my dad's house and demanded anything from him, it became my concern. And that of my boys here." TJ looked at her and winked. "You okay, honey? These men upset you?"

"I'm fine, and no, they didn't upset me, they pissed me off." TJ laughed, as did the men with him. "I don't know who might have called you, but I'm pretty sure that William and his son were just leaving."

"Now you see here—"

That was as far as George got before one of the *boys* grabbed him by the throat and held him up off the ground. Chloe was impressed. And it didn't bother her as much as she thought it should have that he might die right now. George clawed at the hand that held him, and it didn't even bother the man holding him. He just held him up with one hand like he weighed no more than her.

When she cleared her throat, everyone turned to her. Things were about to go shit up as her dad used to say. She'd have to do something to defuse this, or there were going to be a lot of hurt people. Mostly the Flynns.

"William, I want you to observe what is happening to

39

your son. Do you noticed the lack of effort on the part of the man holding him?" The man told him her name. "Sterling then. Do you notice that Sterling is not even breaking a sweat? Even though it's obvious that your son is a fat slob?"

"He has a slow metabolism." Chloe just cocked a brow at him. "What's your point? As far as I can see, he's just adding fuel to my lawsuit. I'm going to own everything that he does in about an hour."

"Really?" She turned to the first officer, his face looking dazed and his eyes unfocused. "You see anything going on here?"

"Here?" She nodded and laughed when he looked around. "I don't know what the fuck is going on here. I came out here to be backup, not have the crap knocked out of me and my gun taken. Where is it anyway?"

"I believe a vampire took it. You should be glad that he didn't slice open your throat while he was at it. Or stripped you down to your naked self. He could have done that, you know." The cop put his hand over his cock. "I doubt that he'd have anything to do with your twig and berries, so you can just leave them alone. He might, however, need a nice snack. Are you willing to offer up your throat in the name of taking me to jail on trumped up charges?"

"Hell no. I'm just the low man out there. There isn't any reason whatsoever for me to be killed because some jackass won't sell a building to this guy for no other reason than he just doesn't want to. What's the hold up? And I'll have you know, I never get any complaints about my cock. I got myself more than just a twig and berries, bitch." Chloe pinched her finger and thumb together to show just how little she thought he might be. "You don't know shit. I'm a lot bigger than everyone I know."

"If you say so." She looked up at Sterling. "I think it's time you let him go now, please. While it's doubtful that you could cause him any more brain damage, he might just die and that would be a lot of paperwork for you. Besides, I think, like the rest of them, his brain is at the other end, not in his head but his ass."

When George was standing on his own two feet, she could almost feel sorry for him. The man was a drug addict, an idiot, as well as a fat fuck. But she also knew that for all his bravo, George was a being pushed around by his father a great deal.

"It's time you men left." The cops stood up first and made their way to the cars. They were staggering a little, and Chloe wondered what else had been done to them other than their weapons taken and them being knocked to the ground. When they were gone, Trent stood in front of William and George with his arms crossed over his chest as he continued. "You come here again and threaten my sister-in-law and I will come after you. You know that I can do it, too."

"You threatening me too? Oh boy, this is going to be the best payoff of my life. The great and powerful Calhouns are going to fall." William looked at her before he spoke again. "Honey, you have no idea what sort of shit you've just stepped in."

"Funny, I was thinking the same thing about you." When she made a lunge at him, she laughed when both he and his son fell back off the porch. "Don't fuck with me, William. I was raised knowing how to defend myself against bullies like you."

As the two of them made their way back to their cars, arguing all the way, she held onto the post next to her. Almost as soon as they were out of sight, she felt the world around her just blink out.

41

~~~

Scott watched her closely. He was both pissed off and impressed. No one in his family could believe how she'd stood up to the two men and had come out on top. Nor that she'd fainted dead away like she had. Scott looked over at his mom when she came into the bedroom with him.

"She's fine, you know that, don't you?" He nodded and told her that he did. "Poor thing. Can you imagine how hard it was for her to stand up to those men? You grandda said he'd be crowing about it for years to come."

"Grandda was terrified like the rest of us when she fell over. Had he not caught her when he had, she'd have hurt herself more." Mom sat down on the chair on the other side of the bed. "She's not going to be happy with me. She might even hate me for what I am."

"I don't suppose you're wrong about that. I mean, you have money, a nice house, and a car. You're good looking, I suppose. You take a shower every day. You do, don't you?" He nodded and smiled at her. "Yes, I can see where she'd think you were the worst kind of man for her to fall in love with."

"That's not all of it and you know it." She asked him what he meant. "You know as well as I do that I'm a deviant. A pervert."

"Deviant? My goodness Scott, wherever did you come up with that idea?" He just stared at her. "So? You like things a little different in the bedroom. I'm assuming that's what you mean."

"It is, and you know that it's a lifestyle that isn't for everyone." His mom nodded, then shook her head. "Mom, she might not care for me."

"And she might, too." He wasn't embarrassed talking

42

about his preferred sex with his mom. She'd been the one who had told him to find someone to talk to when he'd been having issues. He'd never told her what sort of issues, but she seemed to understand him on a level that both surprised him as well as embarrassed him at times. "You should let her make that decision when it comes up. And I'm sure it will."

He turned and looked at Chloe while she slept. There was a great deal about her that he didn't know, especially on a more personal level. Joe had gotten him as much as she could find about her financial life, as well as anything she'd been able to find out about the death of Chloe's father. By all accounts, the matter had been left on someone's desk for years now.

Mike Davis had been a good man. A great father to his motherless daughter, and someone that could be trusted with your life. It really was too bad that no one was there to have his back when he died. Chloe had, of course, taken it hard when her dad had been killed, and had spread it all over town that she was going to find the murderer, even if it took her the rest of her life.

The door opened and closed behind him, and he knew that his mom had left. But he was startled to see Joe sitting in the same chair when she spoke to him.

"I've done some digging. And while I was at it, I had someone look into a few other aspects of the police department. They're corrupt, as you more than likely know, but it's more than that. I'm thinking that they're getting some outside money from other avenues as well." He asked her if it was drugs. "No, that would make it better in a way. I think they're dealing in crap that we have only just started to find."

"Christ, what the fuck could it be if it's worse than drugs?" She told him. "Are you kidding me? Hit men? Our police officers are hiring themselves out as hit men? I wouldn't have thought that any of them could have hit the broad side of a barn, much less a target."

"I think it's a scam." He could see that as well. "They might not all be in on this, but enough of them are that we have a problem on our hands. They cannot only kill without consequences, but they're easily bought as well. Case in point, the Flynns."

He had to agree with her on that one. Even Noah, when he'd returned with the guns a few minutes ago, had said that the men there had been on the Flynns' payroll. Scott wondered if there were any honest people in the world anymore. If there were, they were few and far between.

He knew that his family was good. Hell, they'd instilled a code of ethics and a moral compass in them when they were just babies. Scott knew that it was something that few understood and even fewer people practiced. The Calhouns were the type of people that said what they meant and did what they said they would.

"Scott?" He sat up, looking over at his dad now. "Your mom said you zoned out for a moment or two. She's gone down to have Meggie cook you some dinner. And Joe said that you were resting when she left you. Are you all right?"

"Yes. I think so. I was thinking about what Joe told me. I was just wondering if there were many honest people in the world." His dad snorted and said he didn't think there were. "I guess not. I mean, her talking about the police force here makes me wonder what else might be going on right under our noses."

"You'd be surprised." His dad stood up when Chloe spoke. And when she stood as well, wobbling a little on her feet, he went to help her. "I'm okay now. I was...I guess you could say I was a little stressed out."

"Hot damn girl, you sure do have a mouth on you." His dad laughed, and all Scott could think about was her mouth. And what he wanted to do with it. "I sure wish I could have been standing in front of old William when you told him and that kid of his off. My dad, he said that he was as proud of you as he'd ever been of anyone before."

"You and your father should be stood in a corner." That made his dad laugh again. "Flynn, he has it out for you guys, doesn't he? I mean, even before I came in the picture. When I was standing there, I thought it was me, but it's you he hates for some reason."

"Yes. My dad especially. He's always been a good businessman, knowing when to buy or sell. Made us what we are today, I guess you could say. But this thing with Flynn, it's a little darker than that. William and my dad sort of crossed paths even before the thing with the building." Scott asked him what had happened. "Well, it has to do with a pretty little thing called Christine."

"Mom?" His dad nodded. "I don't understand. What does Mom have to do with business deals and buildings?"

"Nothing. But she was the one that William had set his sights on when he first came to town. She had money, you see, and he didn't. So he set about on this mission to make her come to him." Scott thought of the woman that their friend Noah knew that had been killed for much the same reasons. "Your momma, she wasn't having any of it, and about a week after she finally went out with him, just to shut him up, she met me."

"And he blames you for her not being his wife." Chloe shook her head when Dad nodded. "What a moron. I mean, really. Don't men know how to take no as an answer?"

"I'm sure that most don't." Dad stood up then and moved

to the door. "I'm supposed to tell you both that the house is being watched. The pack has been asked to help out. Also, Trent said that if you should go home tonight that he'd like to know. He's sort of worried that the police will pull you over for no other reason than they think they can."

After he left them, Scott leaned back in his seat. Chloe wasn't saying anything so he took the time to look at her. He knew on some level that she was aware of what he was doing, but he didn't know what to say to her. Nothing that wouldn't get him slapped anyway.

"You spoke to me. Out on the porch earlier, you spoke to me. I didn't think that was possible without sex." He wanted to tell her they could have that too, but only said it was the blood exchange. "I see. And whomever you take blood from, you can talk to them like that?"

"Yes. Although, you should also be aware that you can speak to Trent and Joe that way as well should you want to. They're the pack leaders. But don't call Joe the alpha bitch. She doesn't care much for that title." She nodded and closed her eyes. "Are you all right?"

"No. I'm not even close to being all right. I have a boss from hell trying to get me arrested. For what reason, I'm still trying to figure out. I have this guy, you in the event you don't get it, that says I'm his mate, and he can talk to me through this mind link thing. There are police officers out there that would just as soon arrest me as find out the truth, and I'm unemployed. Not that the latter part is anything to be upset about, but it's on the list now." He asked her if she liked making lists. "Yes. What is it? You have a problem with lists too?"

"No. I have my own list system that I use." He stood in front of her and was glad when she didn't back away. "My list for you would start something like this. A kiss first. Not a deep one, but one that would let me get a taste of you. Then I'd remove your blouse. Slowly at first, then perhaps just rip it from you when I got greedy. Your bra would also have to go. And that I would take off you, peeling it away from your skin and tasting each inch of you as I went."

"What makes you think I want any of that from you?" He could smell her and let his nose fill with her scent. "You're not going to manhandle me, are you? I don't think I could take one more man thinking they can toss me around like I'm nothing but their slave."

Had she hit him, it wouldn't have been any less painful for him. When he backed from her, not touching her, he thought of what she'd said. And he knew, as surely as they were together, that they'd never pair up when it came to sex. As he took another, then another step back, he felt his heart crumble in his chest.

"This was a mistake." She didn't move, but he was all right with that. At least sort of all right. "I'm sorry to have said those things to you. I'll...you should stay here with my grandparents. I'm going to head home."

When he turned and left her standing there, he told his wolf that it was for the best. That she would never get used to something like him. Even as he made his way down the stairs and out of the house, he kept telling himself and the wolf in him that she would be safe here. Shifting even as he leapt over the fence that divided his land from his grandparents', he knew no one would bother her so long as his family was around. Scott was all the way to his home when he realized that he'd not told his grandparents that he was leaving.

CHAPTER 4

Chloe wasn't sure what she was pissed off about, but she had an idea that she wasn't going to get over it anytime soon. As she tried her best to pay attention to the couple in front of her, all she could think about was that Scott had just left her there.

"He didn't do a single thing he said he would to me either." She realized her mistake the moment someone laughed. James and Jasmine had opened their home to her, and she had just embarrassed herself in front of them again. "I'm sorry. I was thinking about something."

"Scott?" She nodded and said again that she was sorry. "Don't be. I'm a little ticked off at him myself. When I asked him why he'd left in such an all fired up hurry, he said that he remembered he had things to do. Seems to me a man has a pretty mate here, he should stick around and talk to her about it."

"He's not happy with me being his mate, I don't think." James only laughed and she looked over at Jasmine. "Scott is a very handsome man. I'm sure he has plenty to do on a Friday night."

"Not like you think. He's embarrassed is all." She asked her about what. "You might want to have this conversation with him, child. He's a little upset that we even know about it. While I can understand his embarrassment, I just don't think he should be."

"You mean the sex clinic? I know that he had it. Why would that embarrass him? And for that matter, why does he even care that I know?" When James laughed again, she wanted to get up and hit him. "You are not helping right now. I'm trying to figure out what I did wrong."

"You didn't do a thing wrong. I guess, first off, that he might not know you have any idea that he worked there. I guess a lot of people do know about it, but not that our Scott owned and operated it." She thought of all the things she'd heard about the place. The kinds of things that people she knew did when they were members. It had only just occurred to her that he might be the same Calhoun that was the one who they said was the owner. "He's afraid for you to find out."

"That he owned this shop, or is there something more?" She felt her face heat up when Jasmine told her there was more. "You mean he actually teaches some of the things to people. As in he shows them how to have sex with ropes and things."

"Yes." There was so much loaded in that single word that she wanted to get up and run from it. But at the same time, she was curious as well. Not about what he did to the other people there, but how one got into such a business. Then it hit her.

"He likes...." She thought of when she asked him if he was going to manhandle her. She'd been afraid, yes, but she'd not meant it in that way. She only meant was he going to harm her, as George had. "Scott plays."

"I would guess that's what it's called, yes." She looked at Jasmine when she spoke. "I don't know a great deal about it. I mean, I love Scott to pieces, but that is something I'd rather not speak about with my grandson."

"No kidding." Chloe was trying to think of things she'd heard. What this one friend of hers had told her about the place. "He's had some trouble there. Lately I mean. Someone hurt a woman in his place, and he shut the doors for good."

"Yes. About a month ago now, I guess. This man, I don't remember his name, he came in under the guise of needing help with his underling." Chloe told her it was a sub. "Yes, that's it, his sub. But apparently he'd kidnapped her or something, and was there to use the equipment that Scott had to abuse her. There was this big fight and he decided that he'd had enough."

As they changed the subject to something less sexual, she thought of Scott. And his list. She'd been making one of her own, one that involved hurting him in different parts of his body. Standing up and helping clear when dinner was over, she thought of him talking to her. Well, he was about to get an earful about not explaining himself, and leaving her here like she wasn't smart enough to understand him. Thinking of Sterling and the way he'd lifted up George, she wondered if Scott would do that to her if she pissed him off enough.

You bastard. What the fuck do you mean by getting me all hot and bothered by stripping me down to my bra, then running off at the last fucking minute? Did you really think that I'd be...? I don't know, appalled by whatever it is that was running thought your thick head? I am so angry with you right now that I could go to your house and beat the shit out of you. She felt his laughter and

51

that got her going more. *You think this is funny? You left me here, with your grandparents to explain to me that you like to play it rough. Well, did you ever think I might like that too? Oh no, you had to run off with your tail between your legs like some little baby that got his feelings all hurt. Well, you'd better bet that I'm pissed off, you little shit.*

I can hear that. There was something odd about his voice. *This is Sterl. And I can tell that you are pissed off. You might have thought of the wrong little shit when you started to talk to him.*

Oh my God. He laughed again. *I'm so sorry. I was thinking of how you lifted that guy up by his neck, and was worried that Scott would do the same to me. I'm so sorry.*

Don't be. It's nice to know that you can stand up to him, so long as it's him next time. She wanted to crawl into a deep hole and never come out. *You should know two things right now. Firstly, he can't hurt you. Not that I know that much about his lifestyle when it comes to sex, but I can only assume that his sort of pain to you won't be the same.*

I know nothing about it either. I have a friend that used to go to his clinic. Sterl said that his brother had a lot of clients that he helped. *I heard. The second thing?*

He's his wolf in the woods behind the house you're in. He has it in his head that he can protect you from a distance. She asked Sterl if he would come into the house. *Not if he can help it. He's pretty sure that you're going to hate him.*

She sat there for several minutes after thanking Sterl for his help. Scott was her mate. While she knew what that meant—she'd known a few shifters in her life—she wasn't really sure how it worked. They loved hard, Chloe knew that, and forever. But that was about it. Also, her friends had told her that the sex was often and incredible.

"Incredible. What is that anyway when it comes to sex?"

When she realized she was talking to herself, a habit that she'd had for a long time now, she went out onto the deck that surrounding the entire house. "Can you hear me, Scott?"

She waited for a full minute before she called out again. And when he came out of the woods about a hundred yards from where she was, she stepped off the deck and into the yard. He didn't come any closer, and she was kind of glad that he didn't.

"You hurt me." He lowered his huge body to the ground but said nothing to her. "You knew that too, I think. Yet you just left me here to deal with this on my own. Is it because you hate me too? Or do you have some other reason for treating me this way?"

I don't hate you. She could hear the anger in his voice. *I'm not mate material. I've some idea that once you figure out what kind of person I am, you'll think so as well. I'm an abusive person by nature.*

"I'd like for you to come closer, please. I feel foolish talking to you across the lawn. Please?" She wasn't sure he was going to come up to her, but he finally did. And when he was close enough for her to touch, she smacked him as hard as she could on the nose. "That's for acting like a big baby."

That fucking hurt. She said she certainly hoped so. *You hit me. You're not supposed to be able to hurt your mate.*

"Well, since you've decided all on your own that you and I aren't mates, I guess that rule is now stupid. What the fuck did you think I was going to do when I figured out, with the help of your poor grandparents, that you were into bondage?" He sat down beside her when she sat on the steps to the deck. "You should have at least talked to me. Leaving me here all alone with strangers wasn't right. Not that I know you any better, but you could have at least explained to me what you

53

thought."

And how would you have taken it, Chloe, if I had told you that I'm a Dom that likes his sex hard and rough? That the thought of tying you up not only makes me hard as stone, but it also makes my wolf hungry for you? She didn't say anything to him, not that he gave her much of a chance. *And while I have you there, your body spread out before me, that I didn't let you come. That I would like more than anything in this world to put clips on your nipples until they burn with pain. I'd like to have you suck on my cock while I stood over you with a whip, hitting you with it hard enough to make welts on your body.*

"Is this true or are you just going for shock value?" He said it was all true. She sat there looking out over the vast yard, the pool, and pool house, without really seeing it, but on some level knowing that they were nice. "If I was honest with you, and I'd really like to be all the time, I'd tell you that I'm turned on by the thought of you doing these things to me. But I'm also a little afraid. I don't know if I could just leap into something like this. I'm not sure how good I'd be at it, not even sure that I'd like it. But you never gave me a chance. Not even a little one."

I was wrong to do that. I'm profoundly sorry. When he put his head on her lap, she rubbed her fingers through his fur. *I'd like to tell you something else. Something that I've never shared with my family, or even the few friends that I have.*

"All right. But I'd like to say something first. Tell you something, I guess. I'm not like other women. I don't do shopping sprees. I don't have a lot of clothing or shoes. If I don't need it or can find several uses for something, then I don't buy it. I have money from when my dad died, but I've never spent it. I decided, a long time ago, that one day I was going to see the world, and I'm going to do it. It's why I quit my job, to take a trip that my dad and I never got to make." Stretching out her legs and letting out a long breath, she finished. "There is a house too, that was his that I still own, and it sits empty right now. A home that I doubt I'll ever live in again. There are just too many memories that hurt when I have to go there. The reason I'm telling you this is if this thing between us doesn't work out, or you decide again to just up and leave me, then I won't want anything from you. I have a way to support myself."

I can live with your habits and shopping. In fact, I think I could fall in love with you for those simple reasons alone. She nodded. *That's what I wanted to share with you. I never thought I'd find a person like you in my life. Since I figured out that I had to have sex in a certain way, with a certain kind of person, I thought I was going to have to...not end my life, I think, but cheat myself to be happy. With you...with you, Chloe, I think I could be happier than I've ever been. Even if you don't care for sex the way I like it.*

When the wolf moved off her legs, she thought that he was going to leave her again. It was painful to be rejected, but nearly too much when it was done by the same person twice. But before she could stand and go back into the house and then on to her own life, Scott was standing over her with his hand out.

~~~

Scott was nervous. And a little afraid. He'd hurt her... he knew that. While he'd been sulking, as his brother called it, in the woods just now, he realized that he'd not given her any kind of clue as to why he'd left. Not only that, but he'd been stupid. Sterl laughed at him for a good five minutes after telling him that Chloe had accidently contacted him and how pissed she was. Letting out a long breath, he knew that right now, this was the moment that either brought them together or tore them apart for good.

"If you take my hand in yours, I promise you that you'll never regret it. I'll take care of you, love you too. If you'll allow me, I'll teach you, slowly, how to enjoy the kind of sex that I like. And if you don't, if for any reason you decide that it's not for you, then I'll back off. I'm out of a job but have been offered one, as enforcer for my brother Trent. Which I think I'll be okay at now." She nodded at him but hadn't taken his hand. "I'm glad that you aren't the frivolous type of woman. I'm not that sort of man either. I have my home only because Trent offered me a good deal. I have money in the bank because I'm too cheap to spend it on things. When you come to my...our house, you'll see what I mean."

"You have no furniture." He nodded and told her some. And some toys. "These toys, you mean the ones that you used in your clinic and not a railroad set." The burst of laughter from him made her smile, and he grinned larger at her.

"No, not a railroad set." He wanted to explain more about it, but he didn't want to overwhelm her right now. "I have a five-bedroom house, not a home. I tried to make it a home, but as a single man, it wasn't working. I've been doing work on it, slowly and without much in the way of progress. I'm easily distracted, I guess. I should have had it done a while ago. Or perhaps I was just waiting on the right person to help me with it."

"Don't get ahead of yourself just yet. My father's home is large too. Six bedrooms with baths. In his spare time, Dad tinkered." He asked her what she meant. "Dad worked on his home, making it larger, putting in the extra baths, and enlarged some of the other rooms. He died before a few of the rooms were finished. He also liked cars. Old ones that he'd get cheap and sell large. It's what funded the house projects for so many years."

"I'm sorry about your dad. Joe—you've met her—she's looking into why his death was never solved." She said that the police had shoved it under the rug and weren't working on it at all. "No. They're not. And you're right about it being shoved away. Joe said she had to use some of her magic to even find the file. The police force has problems."

"No shit." She still hadn't taken his hand, so he took hers. It was that or beg her to take it. "I'm not sure this will work out between us, Scott. You're not honest with me and I need that. I've been lied to enough, by people that I was supposed to trust."

"I wasn't honest or very forthcoming with you. And I'm sorry for that. But I promise you that from now on, I will be. About everything." She nodded and he pulled her body to his. "I want to take you home, to our home. I've contacted my brother and Trent is going to give us an escort to our house. He thinks that Flynn and his merry men are waiting for us to get out where he can get one or both of us."

"You want me to go to your house?" He told her he did, more than anything. "All right then. But as I said, I'm making no promises that I'll stay."

"I can live with that. But know that I'm going to do everything within my power to make you want to stay with me." As they made their way across the lawn, he reached out to Trent. *We're headed to my house now. Through the woods, so if you have pack on the land, can you let them know? She's jumpy enough right now, and I don't want to give her any more reasons to not trust me.*

I have already. Some of them can see the two of you and have already let me know. Have the two of you worked it out? By the way, she has one hell of a temper. Scott asked him if he'd spoken to Sterl and he said that he had. *Christ, I never thought of this until just now…she spoke to Sterl. I swear, Trent, the women of this family are making their own rules as they go along.*

Pretty much. And to be honest with you, I don't think I'd have it any other way.

He was still laughing when they closed off the connection. As Scott helped her over the fence that bordered the two lands, he told her what Trent had said.

"Sterl told me that I couldn't hurt you. Maybe that means that we're not really mates after all." He pulled her to his body, let her feel every part of him. His cock stretched and became painful, his body hard in response to hers. "You have a wonderful body. I love how it feels against mine. But this proves nothing; you know that, don't you? It just means you want sex."

"I *do* want to have sex with you. No, that's not right. I want to make love to you. And I can smell you. Your scent is strong and lovely to us. My wolf, he feels you here as well." She looked up at him and reminded him about honesty. "I am being honest with you, Chloe. Nothing would satisfy me more than to take you home with me and make love to you. Then in the morning when we can move again, I'll show you my play room."

As they made their way across their yard, he pointed out things that were in progress. The pool house was in good shape but needed a paint job. The roof needed to be replaced on the barn. There were all kinds of things in the barn, including an old car that he and his granddad had started redoing a few months ago. There were places for cows or horses that he was eventually going to convert to storage units for things like holiday decorations, as well as a place to put in a sauna.

"Big plans. Do you have a plan to actually finish any of

these, or are they going to be works in progress until I have to go out and do them on my own?" He laughed and said that he did have big plans, but it was getting them done that tripped him up. "I love to work with my hands. Taking things apart, seeing how they work, then putting them back together."

Taking her into his house made him nervous. He knew what it looked like. But seeing it through her eyes made him realize how much he'd undertaken and not finished. There were large rolls of wire in the living room. Panels of glass in the dining room that he was going to use to front his cabinets. Not that the house had been in bad shape when he'd purchased it from Trent, but when he'd decided to expand the living room, he'd found that the wiring wasn't up to code. From there it had spiraled out of control to the kitchen and dining room and remodeling them. He explained to her what was going on.

"I thought I'd have more time to do it now that I'm not working. But I kept getting side tracked. No, that's not true. I was feeling sorry for myself and I just didn't do it." Chloe still said nothing. "I can have someone come in and finish it now. What would you like done to it?"

"Take me to your room." He just stared at her, wondering if she meant his playroom or the bedroom. The thought of either one of them had him all tied up in knots. "Scott, did you hear me?"

"Yes. I'm trying to understand." She asked him what he meant. "I don't know, to be honest. The bedroom is down the hall. But if you mean the room the equipment is in, it's on the lower level."

He watched her face. Scott decided right then and there he'd never bet against her in a game of cards. Whatever she was thinking, however her mind was working, he couldn't see it. Yes, he could feel her turmoil, but not see it on her face. Christ, no wonder she was considered a good cop. You never knew if she was ready to kill you or not.

"I'd like for you to take me to the lower level." He nodded, still not moving. "Don't you want me there? I mean, I know I said I don't know anything about this, but if you'd rather I didn't—"

"It's not that. I want you there more than anything. I guess.... Well, I guess I'm sort of afraid now. Of what you might think. I understand that this isn't a lifestyle for a lot of people, but it's my life and I don't want you to leave me because it might be too much. Do you understand?" When she started moving toward the living room, he was sure she was leaving him. But when she asked him again where it was, he pointed to the door that led to the lower level and his play room. "Chloe, this isn't necessary. You know that, don't you?"

"I know a great many things, Scott. And one of the ways I learn things, in this case what I want or don't want, is to explore." She grinned at him, her entire body looking sexy and playful at the same time. "Do you want to explore with me, Scott?"

They made their way down and he waited while she moved around the room. A lot of things were still in the boxes they had been delivered in, but a great deal had been opened already. He'd set up a few things, the cross and the bar, because they'd been easy, but the rest he'd left alone. Looking at the room, he knew that it would take a great deal more work to get the larger pieces, the ones that he hadn't sold when he'd gotten rid of his building, put together.

"Some of these things, I know what they are. Not really sure how they are to be used, but I know their names." He nodded as she touched the bondage bed then moved to the whipping bench. With everything she touched, he felt his cock stretch more and more. When she opened the cabinet that he'd stocked up with supplies that hadn't been used at the clinic, he had to cup himself. "You have quite a selection."

"I wanted to make sure that when someone came to me with a problem, I could help them." She told him she knew that. "You mentioned to someone that you had a friend that came to see me. So you know, I don't know anyone's names nor would I tell you if I did. It's personal to them and me. But I'd like to know, did he say he learned anything from me?"

"I know that as well. Yes, my friend, he said that you helped him a great deal. Sadly, his partner didn't care for the lifestyle, I think you call it, and left him shortly afterwards. He said he was happier now; it was a sore spot for the two of them, apparently." She pulled out the smallish whip that was made of the softest leather and ran it over her cheek. "Do you want me?"

"Yes." He moved toward her slowly, not sure that he was all that steady on his feet just now. "I'm going to try my best to do this slow for you. Right now, all I can think of is taking you hard, making you suffer. But I can tell you now, you'll enjoy this all the more for it."

"I think so, and I want that too." His cock hurt. So did his head. So many images were running through his head at the moment that he could hardly sort them out. "Where do we start?"

Start? He could only think of the finish line. Her on her knees in front of him. Her backside pink from his hand. Small hurts along her breasts where he'd whipped her. Nipples pink with the release of his clips. When she said his name, he blurted out the first thing he thought of.

"Rules. You need to learn the rules." She nodded and sat

down on the bench. "Christ, you're making me crazy. Rules. Okay, you need a safe word."

"It's supposed to be something that I can remember and that I'd not just say all the time, correct?" He nodded. "Ginger. I don't care for the smell of it, but love the taste in food. Ginger."

"All right." He had to keep telling himself that she was new to this. That even though she might have agreed to playing with him, she might not totally understand what she was agreeing to. "When we're in here, I'm the master. You will only speak when I give you permission. You will do what I say without question. Today will be a sort of learning curve for you, so I'm going to allow you to ask me things you might not understand. Also, and this is important, you are not to keep going when you are no longer enjoying anything that we might do in here. I don't want you hurt in that way. Okay?"

"Yes. I have questions now. If that's okay. This equipment, all of it, it's for your pleasure?" He told her it was for both of them. "I'm not sure if I understand how that is to work then. You're the one that is going to be doing all of this to me so that you can enjoy this, but all I can think of at the moment is how afraid of it I am. Is that normal?"

"Yes, it's new to you and to me with you. I didn't participate when I was teaching. Just guided. Having you in here, with all the things that I've collected, it makes me a little nervous as well. Here's how it works. I'm going to be doing all the work physically. But let me tell you, Chloe, you're going to be doing a great deal more mentally. You'll physically be challenged, but the reward for you, for us, is going to be amazing." He could tell she was still a little skeptical, but he was going to show her how what he was saying was right. "For now, we're going to start slowly."

Having her stand still, he stripped her of her blouse and pants. Leaving on her panty and bra set was difficult for him. Scott wanted to taste every inch of her. Lick parts of her that would reward him so nicely. He had to keep telling himself, slow. Don't rush. She's new to this.

When she was standing in front of him, just in the prettiest dark green underthings, he stepped back. He drew in a deep breath and regretted it immediately. She was wet and aroused.

"You're beautiful. And you're perfuming the air around you so nicely that I want to taste you." Her face reddened and he smiled at her. "Before we begin, I want to tell you something, something I meant to before. I'm truly sorry for everything. I've been...well, I guess in a funk of late. I feel like a failure on all sorts of levels, and I think I took it out on you."

"You did." He didn't know what he had expected, but it was not for her to be so honest with him. But she had warned him that she wasn't going to lie to him. Scott laughed. "Perhaps, even though I have no idea what I'm doing here, I can play with you."

Nodding, he took another step back from her. He had no idea why he was agreeing to this. It was his room, he was the Dom. But he thought that she had it right. Maybe he did need someone to play with him for a change.

CHAPTER 5

Having Scott sit down on the bench behind her, she started unbuttoning his shirt. Her fingers felt like they were all thumbs, but she managed to get his shirt opened eventually, even if a few of his buttons were sacrificed. When he put his hands on her hips, she asked him, politely, to not touch her yet.

"I'm not trying to be bossy. I just don't want to be rushed. And when you're close to me, it's very difficult to think. You touching me sends me into another plane of need." He swallowed twice; she watched his Adam's apple bob up and down with it. But when he nodded, she continued with what she was doing. "My friend told me that it's not so much about pain as it is control. You control all movements of the play, and he thought that was the greatest part about it."

"That's right. Not just control of you, but everything about it. I don't keep you from coming at all, but controlling when you come and how you come will give you a release beyond anything you've ever experienced before." She told him she'd never come before. He grabbed her hands and looked at her.

"I don't believe that."

"It's true. I've had sex, and while it was really good, it was never all that fulfilling for me. I don't blame the men. Mostly it was me. I think I went into having sex with them for all the wrong reasons." He asked her what they were as she pulled his shirt off his shoulders. "Relief, I guess, which was never there for me. Sometimes it was because I was lonely. Since my dad was murdered, I get that way a lot."

"I'm sorry. I'll make sure that you're never lonely again." She wasn't sure how he thought that was going to work. Sometimes even in a crowded room she was lonely, she told him. "I'm sorry love, I truly am. I don't want you to ever feel that way again. And while I know that you have no control over that feeling, if you tell me, I'll help you. Please, tell me what you're thinking."

"When my father was murdered all those years ago, I went into a deep hole. I wasn't sure if coming out of it was an option. Then the police seemed to drag their heels on finding the person. So I left that job and went to find me something where I could work on finding out not only who did it, but why as well. That's how I wound up at the computer store. I had a thought that George was somehow involved. But since then I've changed my mind. If he was the one that killed dad, then William helped him get away with it." He asked her what she'd done for a living before. Laughing, she told him. "I was a cop. And a damned good one too. Not like those guys at the station house now. My dad was one, and I saw no reason to stop—"

He grabbed her hand when she pulled his tee shirt up to his chest. "You were a cop? I mean, really a cop?"

"Yes. And so you know, I'm not sure how I feel about the look you're giving me right now." He nodded and grinned at her. "I don't know why, but that sort of scares me a little."

"Joe is looking for someone to take over the police commissioner job. Someone to go in and clean up the mess that we have there now. I don't know if you...why are you saying no already? You don't even know what I was going to say." She shook her head. "Also, there will be several jobs opening in the other departments when she's finished."

"I don't think so. I can't talk about it right now. Not yet. Maybe when I find the man responsible, but not right now." Standing behind him, she ran her fingers over his shoulders and down over his chest. "Close your eyes for me. I want to give you a massage."

What she wanted to do was think. About anything but being a cop again. As she dug her fingers into his tight muscles, she let her mind think of what she was doing and not what he'd said to her. His muscles began to loosen, but her own body was getting warmer, her need getting stronger. And when he put his hands on hers and pulled her around to face him, she could see his wolf there too.

"Lay down over this bench. My wolf, he needs his mate." Shaking her head, she started to back away. "He wants only to taste you, see if you taste as good as you smell. He wants to drink from you before I do."

"I thought...well, I guess you can guess what I thought. He's not going to have sex with me, is he? Ever?" He shook his head and smiled at her, and she felt it warm her from the inside out. "Scott, is this normal? I mean, that your wolf wants me?"

"Oh yes. Very much so. And while I have never done this to another woman before, I know that it's done between mates." When she was settled on the bench he'd been on, she felt ridiculous. First of all, she was spread out like a dinner party food item, and she was nearly naked. Then Scott pulled out a knife and ran it along her thigh. "These have to go, I think."

The cutting of her panties made her pussy soak. And when he put the blade up under her bra between her breasts, she was panting. Every part of her was ready. For what, she wasn't sure, but she was ready for it. When he cut through the material that held her breasts, she felt her nipples tighten more and her breasts swell.

When he got down on his knees beside her, she reached out to touch him. But he put her hands up over her head and wrapped them around the bar that was there. He never spoke. Chloe knew that her training had begun, and did as he instructed her to do without question.

"When I shift, it's going to be scary. I know you've seen my wolf before, but he'll be aggressive with you. As I want to be. Nod if you understand." She nodded, keeping her eyes on him. "With him, you may come as often as you wish. Don't touch either of us. Understand?" She nodded again. "When he's finished, I'm going to eat you. Fuck you with my fingers until you satisfy me. You are not to come until I say you can. Understand? You may ask questions now."

"What happens if I come?" He rolled her gently to her side and swatted her ass hard. It burned enough that she felt tears fill her eyes. Breathing in her nose and out through her mouth slowly, she knew better than to say a word. This was on his terms. And incredibly enough, she enjoyed that. When he asked her if she had any more questions, Chloe told him no.

The shift from man to wolf was beautiful. He was simply gone, and in his place was the biggest wolf she'd ever seen. Not that she'd seen all that many, but like before she was pretty sure that he was larger than normal. And when he nudged her legs apart, it was on the tip of her tongue to tell him no, that she'd changed her mind. Scott must have sensed her fear, and spoke to her in gentle but firm tones.

You have your safe word; use it now if you want. She shook her head. *All right. Just remember, I won't hurt you without pleasure, and if you need me to stop, as soon as you say the word, it's over.*

The wolf touched his nose to her hip, then her belly. It was cold, as she had expected, but his breath was warm, almost hot. He never rushed her, even though she could almost feel his need to lick her. And when she was ready, or as ready as she'd ever be, she opened her legs wider for him.

His tongue was rougher than she'd thought it would be. Not only that, but it was thick and long. She kept waiting for him to hurt her for some reason, and when she came, a climax that simply took her breath away in its beauty and release, it took her by complete surprise. Not just how hard she came, but how her body was ready for more.

Every time he touched her clit with his tongue, she tried her best not to scream. This was practice, she kept telling herself. When Scott took her she'd not be able to speak or scream. But the more aggressive the wolf got, and he did, the more her body demanded that she let out her release, not just with her body but verbally as well. And just when she thought she'd had enough, that she couldn't come again, Scott was standing over her. Naked.

He looked good enough to devour. Not just for him to come in her mouth, though she thought he'd be delicious, but she wanted to taste him, nibble at his flesh like his wolf had hers. She found herself tempted to touch him, just to see if the burn on her ass was as wonderful as she thought it was. At his order, she stood up. Swaying slightly, she nearly fell over when he bent her at the waist and slammed his cock deep into her pussy.

It was painfully wonderful. He filled her. His cock was thick, and she knew that she was going to be sore from the treatment. But Chloe also knew that the way he was taking her, the pain that was being assaulted on her flesh, was going to give her the greatest reward of all time. Holding on to the bar under her fingers as tightly as she could, she tried her best to think of anything other than coming.

Scott fucked her hard. And holding onto the bench again, she had to bite both her lips to keep from screaming. It was painful. But Christ, it was wonderful too. Reaching up to hold her nipple in her hand, she felt the burning sting of his hand again.

"Did I tell you that you could touch yourself?" She wanted to beg him to hurt her again, to slap her once more so she could come. "Answer me, slave."

"No." He asked her *no* what. It took her lust filled mind a minute to understand what he was asking her. "No, Master."

His cock continued to pound her. Chloe could almost feel it at the back of her throat, it was so deep inside of her. And when he pulled out slowly, his tip filling her entrance, she wanted to back up, take him deeper again, when his hand came down on her ass.

"Don't move." She couldn't if she wanted to. Her body was on the edge of a climax, and one move from either of them was going to send her over. "I love the way my hand shows up prettily on your ass. I can see each of my fingers where I've branded you."

He fucked her slowly now, his cock going in as deep as he could, then pulling out until just the crown of him was inside of her. He did this for hours, it seemed like. Her body was

70

aching for some relief, any relief. When he curled his fingers into her hair and yanked her upright, she did scream at the pain.

Scott didn't move. His cock was still deep, his fingers wound tightly into her hair, and she heard him speaking, but didn't understand a word he was saying. Finally, when the pain of it started to subside, she nodded when he asked her if she was all right.

"What is it?" Tears filled her eyes and she knew that if she told him, he'd be pissed again. "Chloe, I didn't mean to hurt you, but I think it's more than that. I can smell blood."

"He hit me—George did—and I fell and hit my head. I didn't tell the police because…well, I was afraid actually. I've known for some time that his dad has been paying them off, and I didn't want to be arrested too." Scott held her as his fingers loosened from her hair. And when he lifted it up and licked along the wound she knew was there, Chloe moaned. "You're not supposed to be making me feel better."

"Hush. You belong to me now. And I'll do with you as I see fit." As his tongue made a path from her spine to her hairline, all she could think of was how his cock was still deep within her. "You taste of warm cognac to me. Dark and rich."

"Scott. Master? Please. You have to stop. I can't breathe." He laughed a little but didn't stop. His free hand was making its way down her belly to her pussy. "I can't hold on now. I've messed up my ability to concentrate."

"Good. I was beginning to think you were going to outdo me." She felt his fingers slide into her pussy, over her clit, until she wanted to scream for him to finish her. "Fucking you like this, I can feel your heat on my fingers. The way your pussy is tight around my cock. When you come for me, Chloe, are you going to hurt me? Will you strangle my cock while I empty inside of you?"

"Please?" He nipped at her ear lobe. Suckled it into his mouth. And when he pinched her clit, his thumb and finger painfully touching her, she screamed out her release as he bit down on her shoulder.

The pain of it was dimmed by the pleasure. And when she came a second then third time with him touching her, she knew he was doing this for her, only her. As he pushed her back to the bench, gently this time, touching her head to the bench, she said nothing, only offered herself to him as he had her.

Scott took her gently, bringing her several more times as he filled her again and again. When he leaned over her, his body pressing hers down more onto the bench, she offered her throat to him. The feeling of his tongue over her pulse made her shiver. The way his teeth grazed her skin had her moaning. And when he bit down, tearing into her tender flesh, Chloe screamed again, this time as the darkness took her.

~~~

George didn't know what to make of his dad today. He was mumbling about money and buildings, but he was also holding a gun while he did it. George figured he'd live a good deal longer if he just sat there with his mouth closed. He was getting pretty good at that too, keeping his mouth shut when he had nothing to offer. His mind drifted to the deal he'd made just that morning.

His dad was going to be dead within the week, and George thought it was the best news he'd heard in a very long time. He'd found it very easy to schedule his father's demise. At the beginning it had seemed far too easy, but then as he made his way through the questions that had been asked of him, he realized that it was going to be a bit more difficult than he'd first thought. First of all, his dad wasn't alone often. Rarely, as a matter of fact. And when he was, it was because he was locked up in a car with a driver, or in his offices like he was right now. His hired gun had leaned back in his seat and shook his head.

"You do know that in order to take him out, we're going to need him to be somewhere that we don't have to kill a dozen people to make it happen." He nodded at the man who had refused to tell him what his name was every time he'd asked him. "Do you think you could name at least one time when he doesn't have someone guarding him?"

"At home in bed. Sometimes he goes and sees this woman who fucks him. I don't know if you'd charge more to kill her as well, but I'd rather not have to pay out anything else." The man just cocked a brow at him. "He doesn't have much in the way of staff when he's at home. Usually this guy named Moody—he told me his name—anyway, Moody goes to the house on the estate before Dad does. He's responsible for securing the house."

He'd had to tell the man his code to get past the guard shack, as well the one on the front door. It had taken nearly two hours for him to find the information that he wanted, and another hour before the guy called him back to tell him whether or not he'd kill his dad. Also, he wanted a deposit before he'd do a damned thing. That had been trickier. He'd had to take a lot of jewelry from his dad's house, stuff he was sure his dad didn't know George knew where it was to pawn to pay the man. Now here he sat with his dad again, listening to him go on about nothing.

"Are you even listening to me?" George tried to focus on his dad, but it was hard after hitting the coke like he had an hour ago. "Are you ever not stoned George? The reason that

I ask is we have a problem on our hands, and you're the one that caused it by letting the only sales person we had working go. What the fuck were you thinking? Or were you? I told you, several times, that we had to stay in business or there would be hell to pay. What if they find out that you killed that cop? If I don't have that building, then that's a good possibility."

"I still don't think that I killed that cop, Dad." His dad only snorted at him and told him he had. George kept thinking about that night, and he was sure as he sat there that he'd not killed anyone. Not that night anyway. "What are you going to do about this woman? I tried to get her to take back her notice, to make her stay, but that guy came in and he took her away. Then I was arrested. That wasn't right, Dad. I didn't do anything wrong but to try and make her stay and work for us. Like you said, those other people haven't any idea how to do their job without her there holding their hands all the time. What if you paid her to come back?"

"The job was only a place where you could go every day and not bug the shit out of me. All you had to do was keep it going and making a little profit. And don't think I don't know where that money went, either. Up your fucking nose." Well, that hurt, George thought. "And if it fails, we're both going to be in deep shit. Deeper than you know. And that doesn't negate the fact that she's in with the Calhouns now. What do you suppose is going to happen when she tells them what a drug addict you are? Not that the entire town isn't aware of it already. But if she does, then how long do you think it's going to be before they figure out you murdered her dad? Not long, I can tell you that."

His father had this unhealthy thing about the Calhouns. He'd tried, several times over the last ten years or so, to get Dad to tell him why the fuck he had a hard on for them, but all he'd ever gotten out of him was that TJ had stolen something from him. And when he'd asked if he could go and steal it back, he'd only slapped him in the face. It was the last time he'd brought the Calhouns up.

"I need to buy that building. And fucking soon." That was another thing he didn't understand. With all the empties all over town, why the fuck did he have to have that one? "The moment that we move out of there, according to our lease we have with that prick, they can do whatever they want to the building. For now, all they can do is collect rent. I cannot let them have access to that building, and now because of you, they'll have all the rights they want. Fuck, this shit is going to get you killed, George."

"Why? Why not just give him more than he paid for it?" His father just looked at him. "Damn it, I don't know why you want it so badly anyway. It's falling down, there isn't a decent place in it to get cooled off, and the bathrooms need to be updated. Twice when I went in the men's room to take a shit, the toilet didn't want to flush."

"That's because you save it all up for a single dump a week, and it's like trying to flush a truck down a toy car system. Why can't you just go at home?" George said he didn't care for the way it smelled. "Well, you can bet your bottom dollar that the people who work for you don't care for it either. And the reasons I want that building are none of your concern. He got me when we were down, and he won't let me have it back for any amount I throw at him. So you just keep going to work there so that we can keep renting it."

After he left his dad's office, George made his way to his suite of rooms. He supposed it was frowned upon to still be living at home at thirty-five, but he didn't want to have to be bothered with rent. And besides, he was pretty sure that no one would rent to him again. He'd had too much fun at his last place.

George went to his closet and pulled out the briefcase he'd stored in there several weeks ago. Over the last few months he'd been collecting the rent money from the electronics building that his dad had given him and storing it away. When he realized that something might happen to it at the office, he'd gotten himself a nice leather briefcase and had been putting it in it. Taking it home with him had been tricky too. He'd had to find a way to hide it in his room so that none of the snooping staff found it. Finally, he'd told them to stay completely out of his personal space.

It never occurred to him that his room would suffer from them being banned from his place. His bed was never made now, and he couldn't remember the last time that his towels had been refreshed. He supposed there was a linen closet around someplace that he could get some clean ones from, but again, he didn't want to bother. He was going to own this house soon, and then there would be changes all the way around. First and foremost, he was going to move into the master bedroom and piss all over his Dad's bed before having it removed. George wanted the bigger bed, not the small king he had now.

George had over sixty grand in his case. Nearly all of it was the rent money that should have been paid to the Calhouns. And he'd begun taking money from the drawers at the end of the night as well and not making a deposit. It wasn't as if his dad couldn't afford the loss of money, but he would be pissed if he knew. His dad was a stickler about things like money, especially lately.

Putting the cash away again after taking out enough for a hit or two, he put on some reasonably clean clothing and made his way down the stairs again. His dad was going out the door, so George paused at the landing to wait until he was gone. George didn't have time to get into any kind of fight with him again. He had things to do, and his dad was just too judgmental. He saw Claude, the butler, go to the door with him.

"Sir, there is a phone call for you. Mr. Calhoun would like to speak to you about the building you're renting from him." Dad told him to tell the man to fuck off. "I'm sure that I can't do that, sir, but you should know that he claims you to be in breach of contract."

"What sort of breach, did he say?" Claude said that he had not. "Just tell him that we're going to be there until computers are out of style. And we both know that that's not going to happen. Tell him…I don't care what you tell him, but I'm going out the door to a business meeting. If he has any questions, tell him to talk to my attorney."

After his dad left, George made his way down the stairs. Claude was still standing there, looking at him as if he were a dangerous bug. He'd better be nicer to him, was all George could think of. Soon he was going to be running this place.

"Mr. Flynn, I was wondering if there might be a chance that we can tidy up your room. The staff has noticed that there is a vile odor coming from in there." George said nothing as he gathered up his coat and hat. Winter was coming on hard now, and he was never sure he'd get a ride back to the house. "Also, there is the matter of your laundry."

"My laundry? What about it?" Claude said that there hadn't been any in some time. "No shit. It's all over my room. And as for the odor, I don't smell a damned thing. Stay out of my room, and I'll set my dirty underwear out in the hallway for you to find."

George was going to take a dump in a pair of his finest boxers and set them right on top of all his laundry. Yes, sir, he thought, that'll make a great odor coming from the vicinity of his room. Laughing as he left the house, he waited on the steps for the limo to come around. He had called down to the garage before he'd left, and hated that he wasn't where he'd told him to be. Just as he was going to pull out his cell and call down to the garage, it rang.

"I forgot to tell you, your car won't be at your disposal today, George. I've got a lot of errands to run and mine is in the shop." George asked him how that was his problem. "Because I pay the bills and you don't. Why don't you just drive yourself in? It's not like you don't know how. I paid dearly for you to have a license that you no more deserve than you do that check you get every week. There is a perfectly good car in the garage for you to use. Just try very hard not to kill anyone again."

When the line went dead, George wanted to scream. He thought about throwing his phone across the yard, but didn't at the last minute. He would have to beg for a replacement as he'd done last week, and he wasn't going to go through that again. His dad was making everything more difficult. Rubbing his forehead at the pain that was constantly there, he tried to think what he was to do now. He really hated his father.

The car that he could drive was banged up. He'd told his dad several times that it needed to be put in the body shop, but he had yet to have it done. George could not wait for his dad to be dead. Once he was things would finally start getting done around here. All this bullshit of being put off like he wasn't worth it was driving him nuts. Didn't his dad know that your children were supposed to get it all?

George was almost all the way to his job when he remembered that he had to get money to the killer. He loved that…the killer. His dad was going to be so surprised when he had a gun pulled on him or whatever this guy decided to do. George only wished that he could see his face when the guy told him it was from him. It was something that George was going to have to pay extra for, the man telling his dad that George was the one that paid to have him killed. But it would be worth it to know that his dear old dad knew he'd outsmarted him.

His dad thought he was stupid. It wasn't as if George didn't have his problems, he did. But to be called that by your own flesh and blood hurt more. Most of the time, when he'd been just a kid, George would hide from his dad until he realized that Dad preferred it that way, that George wasn't around. Then when George's mom had run off with that man, he'd been shoved away more often. He was pretty sure that his dad wished that she'd taken him with her when she'd left. George did too sometimes.

His dad, he knew, was a prick to everyone. He didn't seem to have any friends that George had ever met…only business associates or an occasional woman that would spend the night. That didn't happen often, however. He thought his dad had the same issues he did with the broads. He was simply too fat for them. His dad was also a liar.

George thought about the death of the cop and knew, way down deep inside, that he'd not had a thing to do with it. It had been, he thought, his dad all along. He was pretty sure that he'd remember something like that. When he was high or drunk and something happened, he would sober up pretty quickly.

Pulling out his cell phone, he texted the killer, telling him that he'd have to get with him later in the night. George also told him that he had a few things to tell him as well, and could they meet for dinner. As he waited for the man to answer him back, George took three more hits off his hand and set up another deal to meet with his dealer.

Fine. For some reason the single word answer back from his hit man made him pissy. But he knew better than to cross the man. Things were about to get hot around here, and having a pissed off killer wasn't going to be conducive to his plans. George could not wait to be in charge of shit.

CHAPTER 6

Joe looked over the file three times before setting it aside. She was pretty good about seeing things where others couldn't, but this file was so full of holes that she wasn't sure what to see and what not to see. It was difficult to understand most of what was written it in as well. It looked to her like the author of the pages had gone out of his way to scribble more than usual. Tanner cleared his throat when she said nothing for several minutes.

"Do you see it?" Joe told him she did not. "That's right. Because it's not there. Nothing is."

"I don't understand this. You told me to look this file over, and now that I have, you're telling me that it's not there. I'm confused." He laughed and made his way to her desk. "You know that I could hurt you right now, don't you?"

"I know that you love me too much to do that. Besides, Noah adores me and would miss me terribly." She snorted. "You're very good at that now too, the snorting thing. I'm thinking you picked it up from Dad. Or was it Mom? She's pretty good at it too."

"Just show me what it is you think I missed. I'm not saying that I have, but show me." He pulled out the form from the coroner with his notes on it. "That's another thing I had here to ask you. Why are there no actually photos of Mr. Davis when he was killed?"

"The report says that there are some. A total of sixteen, as a matter of fact. But when I asked to see them, they said it was part of an ongoing investigation and they were unable to release them just yet." Joe asked him if he thought they'd taken any at all. "I do. I don't know why they won't hand them over for sure yet, but I know that they took them. Somewhere in the file there is a receipt for them. Someone, and I can't make out the name, has asked for them, and it looks like they've never returned them. Could be why they're not able to let me see them with the file."

Joe picked up the form when he showed her which one. It was a list with the date, the file number, as well as the name of the person who handed them out and the person who received them. She looked up at Tanner when she figured it out.

"Chloe has them." Tanner told her that it wasn't possible. "I'm telling you this is her name. C. Davis. She's made it so it's difficult to read on purpose, I think, so no one would be able to see it was her. And I'm betting if there were cameras there, they were disabled as well. She has them."

"But in order to get them, she would have had to be either an attorney or an investigating officer. I don't believe she's either." Joe thought perhaps Chloe was the latter of the two and told him that. "You think she's a cop? But she was working for the computer place. Why would she...? Holy fuck, Joe. You think she knows everything that is going on at the station and quit?"

"That would be my guess. And the only way we're going

to find out is either dig deeper or ask her." Tanner said he thought digging would be easier. "More than likely you're right, but I think asking her will get us a better answer, don't you? She's intense, I get that. More so than I am at times. But there are other times when I think she is as soft as a kitten in her emotions."

Joe thought about Chloe, and some of the things she'd said to her just yesterday. Like how the two officers that had come by the house again were part of the goon squad. She'd asked her what she meant and Chloe had just shrugged. Then last night she'd told Trent that the cops he was talking to could no more be trusted than a snake with a rat. She knew just what was going on at the station, and Joe was pretty sure that she knew who was in charge.

"Do you suppose she'd come here and help us out?" Joe told Tanner that she was on her way over anyway. "You knew before this then."

"No. She's coming over to talk to Sterl about a couple of pieces of furniture at her dad's house. Did you know that she inherited not just his home, but a lot of old furniture and cars?" Tanner said that he knew very little about her. "She's not very forthcoming, yes, but I think that's her personality, not her being rude. I thought she was sort of standoffish, but I'm beginning to think she's just observing everything. I bet she could give you a rundown on any of us that even we might not know about ourselves."

"And that, my dear sister, is just as scary. A cop? I can't believe it. Do you suppose we could talk her into coming and working for the station? Maybe even take the damned thing over? We sure could use a good man in the position." Joe said she'd not push it. "Yeah, she'd tell me no, I'm betting. I think I would as well."

83

The doorbell rang and Joe leaned back in her seat. It was Chloe and she was alone, Joe knew that. No one else would have rang the bell, because they were family and came and went as they pleased. It would take her a while, she thought, to feel like she could be a member of this family. Trust would have to come first. When she was shown into the room with her and Tanner, Joe knew that something had happened. Trent joined them a few minutes later, after the butler came to ask about refreshments.

"I won't be able to stay long. I have to go to the doctor today." Joe asked her what had happened. "The other day when I was in the shop George hurt me, and Scott wants me to have a follow-up exam done so there is a record. It probably won't hold water, but he made me promise that I would."

"I have something to ask you, Chloe. Well not ask, but... you're a cop, aren't you?" Chloe told Tanner that she wasn't. "Maybe not now, but you were at one time. And you left after the investigation of your dad went cold."

Chloe didn't say anything at first. Joe had a feeling she was testing the waters, so to speak. Or thinking of just how to answer. She'd noticed that about her young new sister-in-law...she thought things out before speaking. It was another good trait to have as a cop.

"I believe that George killed my father when he was drunk or high. And that his dad either knew about it or was just as involved. Or perhaps William did it. I'm no longer sure, only in that they're involved somehow." Whatever Joe had expected, that wasn't it. Before she could ask her how she came to that conclusion, she continued. "I also think that William killed his wife, and her body is either in the building that Flynn Computers is in or around it. I've been working there to see if I can find evidence on either murder. There are clues...not huge ones, but enough to make me believe that he's done something with the—"

"Wait. What? You've been under cover working to find if they murdered two people?" Chloe said that she wasn't. Trent looked at her, then back at Chloe before continuing. "You don't work for the police, or you're not looking for the murderer of two people?"

"I'm not with the police department. What I'm doing, I'm doing on my own. And I don't think that Williams's wife is the first person that he's killed, either. Nor, if this thing escalates the way it looks like it will, that they'll be the last if things continue with your family. Desperate men take desperate and oftentimes stupid actions. I understand that you're taking precautions, but this man has an entire department at his disposal. He'll use them to get back at you. Hard." Joe asked her why she quit then. "They weren't doing anything, and it was getting difficult to work at a place as bad as that place is. Besides, I could look around better if I was not employed there. Like, I could get in and out of the lower level of that place without being seen at night. During the day I could never get to the basement and look around like I wanted without someone seeing me. Not to mention—I don't know if you're aware of this, or perhaps you are—the entire department isn't trustworthy. Not only that, but I think most of them are on someone's payroll. Not just the Flynns'."

"I could help you with that." Chloe shook her head at her. "Let me rephrase that. I know someone that can get in and out of there without ever being seen. And he can tell if there is a body down there as well. Where do you think it is?"

"Under the concrete that is.... You mean a vampire." Joe nodded. "I don't think that will work either. I've taken down some monitors, to read odors and such, and it comes up with

85

nothing. They either buried her very deeply, or they used some sort of chemical to get rid of the body before burying her."

"How sure are you that she's down there?" Instead of answering her, Chloe asked to use her computer. As soon as she put the thumb drive in, Joe thought the woman was smarter than anyone had first thought. And Joe thought her to be brilliant already. "You have all the files on here? What about the pictures of your dad's murder? Do you have those as well?"

If she was surprised by the question, she didn't show it. As she clicked through the separate files, some of them named, others just numbered, Joe wondered what sort of commissioner she'd make for this town. Someone to trust, that was sure, but also a person that would get jobs done. And keep the people here safe. The department, or the lack of it, was hurting them by keeping other businesses from relocating here.

"Yes, I have them. The originals are hidden away. Also another copy of this drive. In the event that something happens to me, all this plus the things that I've been able to collect go to the FBI. Not that I'm saying you guys will hurt me, but I'm not into taking any chances." Trent asked her who she had on the force. "No one is to be trusted in the police department. It's big, this thing that they have going on. They'll do some minor things around town. Look into a robbery. Give out a few tickets. But if you were to look into their backgrounds, any of them, you'd see that not one of them graduated from any academy, nor have any of them registered with any of the state or local fire arm groups. In order to carry their weapons, the police are required to register to do it. Also, there is a great influx of money to and from accounts that some of them have.

There are offshore accounts, I'm sure, but I'm not equipped to look for any of those without drawing attention. And for now, I'm just looking, not arresting."

"They're hit men. For organized crime syndicates. Were you aware of that?" Chloe said nothing, but Joe knew that she was aware of it. "All right then, we'll pretend that you answered. Why did William murder his wife? And why do you believe that her body is in the basement of the building?"

Chloe pointed to the computer screen and the four files that were opened. She asked that she open the first one. This file was simply called Deaths. Joe wondered what sort of things this girl had had to do to get all this information, and how long she'd been working on it.

"William's wife's name was Cybil Porter Flynn. She came from an affluent family; only child of a very smart man. They were married about a year after William came to town, and he started tossing money around that he neither had nor would ever have. Then about six years ago she filed for divorce. It really didn't come as a surprise to most people. William was an ass and he didn't care who knew it. Cybil's father hated him. The divorce paperwork has since disappeared, along with her attorney. William has put out there that she ran off with him, and never completed the paperwork because she'd had a change of heart or some bullshit. There was also paperwork that stated that he's not entitled to anything. A pre-nup that he signed when they wed was executed in a way that if anything should happen to her, or to her father, who is also missing, that her husband was to be kicked to the curb. Not her words of course, but close enough." Tanner asked her how she knew this. Using the mouse, she pulled up a copy of not only the pre-nup, but also an addendum to it stating that any children not of her body were to get nothing as well.

"I think she did this, early on in their marriage, after a child other than George was born. She would have known about George; he came to visit them off and on through her life, and for the most part, he does refer to her as Mom. But George isn't her child. And the money doesn't belong to either of them. William made sure that this part of his marriage was never brought up in the courts so that no one would be suspicious about why she was gone."

"She had all the money." Chloe nodded. "And this is why she was murdered. To keep the cash flowing for William to live the lifestyle that he'd grown to love."

"Oh yes. But there isn't that much of it left, at least as far as I can find out. He can't sell the house, not for any reason. The contents are pretty much gone too, as he's pawned or sold off most of what he could. George has pretty much snorted most of his part of whatever the two of them have fixed between them up his fucking nose. And if your grandda doesn't know already, the building downtown is behind in their rent, as well as the gas and electric are close to being shut off. William is hurting too. Bad investments are only the tip of the iceberg on the shit that he's done to get him where he is now." Joe asked her how much. "When they wed the estate was worth just over three billion, and making money pretty fast. But there is also the estate of her dad, who came up missing, and he got that as well. I'm not sure how he got them to declare him dead yet, but with the shit going on in this town, who knows? So the two of them had about fifteen to twenty billion in assets and cash. Now? Maybe a million. Probably less than that, but not more."

"Holy fuck." Tanner said it well, Joe thought. When Sterl and James came in the office to join them, they were brought up to speed on things as well. "And she said that there isn't much in the way of money left after all that."

Joe knew that Chloe knew more. Whatever it was, she could find out by searching her mind, but she didn't want to have to do that. They were family, but Joe was pretty sure that Chloe had her reasons for keeping some of what she knew to herself. And she'd bet anything it had to do with the death of her dad. Then it occurred to her.

"Your father knew all this. You think this is why he was killed." Chloe sat down without answering, but Joe thought she was on to something. She looked at the file folders for the drive and saw the file pictures. Without asking, she opened it up and nearly closed it again when she saw the body. "Christ, he wasn't a hit and run at all, was he?"

~~~

Scott moved the empty boxes outside to the dumpster that had been brought in this morning. He'd gotten a lot done since he'd gotten up…more than he had the entire time he'd been working on the house. Even the yard was beginning to take on a better, like someone actually lived here look.

He paused going into the house when he saw someone coming up the drive. Out of the corner of his eye he saw pack coming from the tree line. The cruiser made him a little nervous now after talking to Chloe late into the night last night.

Three men got out of the cruiser. He wondered first of all why they were piled up in the front seat when another cruiser pulled in behind it. Scott told his wolf to be calm, but it was difficult to keep him under control when all he wanted to do was shift and hurt these men.

"Hey there, Scott. Doing some work, are you?" He just nodded, glad for the four wolves that came closer to the house. "I was wondering if you have permits to do any work on the house. I know that you applied for them, I saw that paperwork, but not that a permit was ever issued."

"The contractor has it. He filed and got the paperwork last week." The cop didn't move from the cruiser and the other two cops moved around the yard, as if they were spreading out. The pack stood behind the second one, but out of sight of all of the men. "You only came out here to check on my permits? Seems a long way to go since I don't live in town."

"Yeah well, we have to make sure that you're not out here just building whatever you want. There are rules, you know." Scott nodded and asked him if he was aware of them as well. "You betcha I am. Got a whole list of them right here in my pocket. How about my partner and I have a looksee around your place? Just to make sure that you're up to code."

"No." The cop just grinned at him and put his hand on his weapon. "You take that from your holster, and before you can even pull the trigger you're going to have your throat ripped out."

The low growl from the wolf closest to the cop made him pause. When he turned slowly, Scott could tell the exact moment that he realized he was outnumbered. There were at least a dozen there now, all of them part of the pack that Trent was taking over. It was then that the second cruiser, this one with only two men in it, emptied as well. All the men had their hands on their weapons, but thankfully no one had drawn them as yet.

"You're not being very friendly, Scott. What would happen if word got around that no cops are welcome out here? What would you do if there was an emergency and no one showed up?" Scott waited for him to turn to him before he answered.

"If I have an emergency, I'm pretty sure I'd do a much better job than any of you would in taking care of it. So now that we've established that you're not only not welcome here, but not going to get in my house, you should leave." Scott had a moment of panic when another car pulled into his drive. But when his mom and dad got out of the car, his mom with her phone out recording everything, he wasn't sure if he wanted to hug them or tell them to get to safety. "Now, for the camera this time, I want you to tell me again that I don't have permits, that you think to come into my house, and that you might not come out here if there should be an issue. Go ahead, my mom would just love to post this on her social media page."

Without another word the cop got into his car, and then the others did as well. Scott wasn't stupid enough to think this was over, so he stood as still as he could. Then the cop rolled down his window and spit at him. It was childish and immature, but Scott didn't care so long as they were all gone. As soon as the cruiser was out of sight, he sat down on the ground where he stood. His dad came to him immediately.

"You all right, son?" He nodded but didn't get up. "Your momma and I thought you'd been hurt when we saw them coming up the drive. Would have been here sooner, but turning around in the middle of the road is not as easy as it sounds."

"Dad, don't let the cops find you alone. Not either of you." He said that he'd make sure that they didn't. "I mean, if they pull you over, don't get out of the car, don't roll down the window, and for God's sake, don't let them in your home. They're not happy with us right now."

"I'm thinking this has more to do with my dad's building than we thought, doesn't it?" Scott told him it was much more. "We need to have us a family meeting. You come on into the house now, and your mom and I will gather the troops. It's past time we get things done here."

Within an hour his house was full. He was glad now that he'd taken the time to get some of the boxes out of the way and had rolled the wire out of the house. The contractors were still working on the kitchen — the wiring there had to be replaced and a few other modifications were being done — but for the most part, the rest of the house was coming along. They were waiting on Randal to get there, as school was out for the day, and Noah. Noah had some information for them as well, it seemed, and was waiting for the sun to set a little more before he arrived.

"You thinking he's found out something about that woman, William's wife?" Grandda had been most upset to know that a body might have been buried in his building. His idea had been to go there and dig her up, to give her peace, but Trent said they had to wait. "I'm understanding that the cops aren't worth a hill of beans around here, but that woman has family someplace. They might want to have her home with them."

"We'll get her home, Grandda, but we have to move like this for the time being. First of all, we don't want them running, and secondly, we have to figure out if they did indeed do it and the other murder." Scott hated to bring her dad up at this time, but he looked at Chloe. "Tell them what you told me, honey. Tell them all of it."

"My dad was investigating the disappearance of David Taft. He'd been a friend of his for years, devoted husband to his ailing wife, and a good man all around. He and my dad would hang out together when they could. And he said that he would never believe that David would run off with a married woman, much less Mrs. Flynn." Dad asked Chloe why her in particular. "Dad said she was a first class bitch. Not a nice person at all. She was a smart businesswoman and all, but not nice about it. Dad thought that was what brought them together. While I guess opposites can attract, these two didn't care for each other on a personal level. But she had used him for the divorce proceedings."

"She was leaving William then. That cock and bull story that he told us all about her running off, it's not true." Trent's statement seemed to spark a lot of questions from the rest of them, but Chloe cut them off when she started talking again.

"Cybil and William had been married about four months when she found out about George. He would have been a teenager or so by then, I think. His being around, as well as the birth of another child born after they were married, but who has since died, were the reasons that her will was changed. David had told my dad that he needed a witness to the fact, and he'd gone over to the office to act as one for them. He told me later that while he didn't care for the woman at all, she'd been screwed over royally by William. She changed her will twice more over the course of the next three years, and each time my dad was a witness to it." Grandda asked what she'd changed the other times. "The second time was to make sure that George got nothing of her estate should she die before William did. She even had the stipulation in the will that if William outlived her that he couldn't give any of the money to his son. Or any other illegitimate children of his. If he did so, then he would lose it all. The money was to go to a charity that she'd set up. It wasn't something that most people would think of as a charity, but the way it had been set up, it qualified. The money was to go to kids in college to be able to afford to have nicer things in their rooms when the college wouldn't provide them. Apparently this was a big deal for her."

"The rich and their money." Scott nearly told his dad that he wasn't a poor man either, not by any means, but he continued. "So you know, I got it set up so that my money goes to a grocery store for the rich and stupid. It'll charge nine times whatever the going cost is for something so that them fools will be broke in a week."

"Hush now. You've done no such thing." His mom smacked his dad on the arm as she looked around the room. "We have it set up so that all you boys get it. Not that we're going anywhere for some time, but there it is. Now, child, tell us what else you've been able to find out. And I have to say, I'm very proud of you for gathering this all up. Very brave of you as well."

Scott hadn't told Chloe that she was an immortal as yet. He'd have to talk to her when everyone left. But she seemed to understand what his dad was saying and looked at him with a cocked brow. He just smiled. Christ, he was in love with this woman.

"Anyway.... Then there was the third time she came to have her will changed. At that time David made several copies of it and had her sign each one. My dad was given one, and the others were filed away in David's office." Noelle asked if she had the copy. "Yes. It's with the photographs of my father when he was killed."

"What did it say this time?" Scott was pretty sure that Tanner already knew. When he had gotten here today, he'd come with Joe and Chloe. "And the changes, did her husband know about them?"

"Yes, I'm sure that she made him aware of them this time. She wanted an extra copy for him, to show him what she was up to. It might have been what got her killed." Tanner asked again what it was. "She cut William out of everything. He would have had to leave the house as soon as she was declared dead, given up all the cars, money. Also, and this

94

was what made it so he'd not be able to sell off the house, he'd no longer serve on the boards of her holdings. The company, the one her father started, owns it. And because of her smart thinking, the company is doing well and making all kinds of money that neither William nor George will ever inherit should her body turn up. I think she might have known she wasn't long for this world."

No one said a word for several minutes. Scott had known all this, but to see the realization on his family's faces, the knowledge that someone they knew could be so hideous, was earth shaking. When he looked at Chloe again, he could see what this was costing her, to bring this up over and over again, and he got up to hold her in his arms. Trent was the first to ask after her dad.

"They claimed he was a victim of a hit and run. But it was more than that, we think. He was also mutilated after the fact. I don't think George would have done the damage done to him, nor William. He wasn't one to get his hands dirty if he didn't have to. But the cops took their time with him, even after he was gone." Joe said she had pictures should anyone want to see them. Scott hadn't thought they would, and wasn't surprised when each of them declined. Chloe continued. "There wasn't ever any kind of investigation. No one looked for a car that he'd supposedly pulled over, nor did anyone have any records of the call in that he made before he'd gotten out of his car. His body was found on the roadside, as it says, but when he arrived at the hospital, nothing was consistent with anything like a car hitting him. The coroner at the time apparently didn't think so either, and took the pictures that I now have. I was afraid, and rightly so, that they'd disappear."

"Why do you think he was killed by George?" Chloe pulled away to answer his dad. And when she handed him a file, Scott was glad when she came back to him. As his dad went over the file, Chloe explained.

"Twenty-four hours after my dad was killed, George was sent away on an extended vacation. His car, a little sports number, was also gone. I know that the car was never destroyed or sold. The VIN number would have had to show up somewhere. I think that it's been taken someplace and hidden away. You see in there, the tests that were run? Those are the chips of paint and glass that were found on my dad's body. With them I was able to figure out not just the make of the car headlights, but also the color of the car and what manufacturer used it. It's consistent with the car that is no longer on the Flynn estate." Tanner asked if she knew where the car was now. "No. I wish that I did. I think I've been able to narrow it down to out of state, and that around that time there was a large sum of money paid out. It nearly bankrupted William's account, but four days later half the money was put back in. I think whoever hid the car is now dead and never collected on the entire amount."

"So this person, he was supposed to get rid of the car somehow and then return for his other half? I'm assuming that he didn't trust William either." Chloe smiled at his mom this time. "You've done some amazing work, child. I do hope we can put it to use."

"I will. If the car was taken to a lot to be crushed, the VIN number, as I said, would have to be recorded. Most places won't touch a car without one. Some will, but most know that its trouble if they do. Also, the same if it was sold to someone. Even without any sort of registration on it, it could be gotten by the VIN the same way...apply and hope that nothing shows up. It has to be hidden away so that no one searches for it." She smiled again. "I think, hope really, that when we

96

do find the car that it still has something on it that will connect the dots to the murder of my dad. Not only that, but William and George's part in it."

"So if you have the car, you pretty much have them dead to rights." She said she only had a theory that William or George got rid of it, nothing more. "But what about the paint and glass? Surely that helps."

"Do you let your own sons use your truck or car? And should they have an accident in it, are you going to assume that they did it?" He said they'd damned better well not have an accident, but he understood. "I need to know without a doubt that William and George conspired to cover up the murder of my dad, and that they also killed their wife and mother."

Just as they were being called to dinner—Scott hadn't even realized that it had gotten so late—Noah showed up. And when he spoke, it was with a great deal of sorrow, Scott thought.

"I've gone to the Flynn Computers as asked. And I'm sorry to inform you that there are bodies in the basement. Good call, Chloe. There is lye covering at least two, but perhaps more, including the surrounding area, but there is cause to think that the wife is there. Not where the new concrete has been poured, but to the left. I would bet that the hole was dug to throw someone off, while the body had been put several feet to the left of the stairs." Noah looked at Scott when he continued. "I should like to talk to you when this is finished, if you don't mind. There is a private matter I have in mind for you."

CHAPTER 7

Randal watched the children as they ran and played. There were times that he wished he could join them. Not only in their fun, but their innocence as well. Children, he thought, had all the right answers. From how to stop fighting to simply the ability to get along. Randal saw the principal coming toward him just as the kids were being lined up to go inside.

"Mr. Calhoun, there's an officer here to see you. He said that your dad has been hurt and that you need to come with him to the hospital. I'm so sorry. You go on ahead now, and I'll take care of your class." Randal reached for his brothers and was told that their dad was just fine. "Your father is such a wonderful man. I do hope he's all right."

"Mrs. Carter, my father isn't hurt." She said that the officer said he was. "No. I just spoke to my brother not three minutes ago, and he would have mentioned that Dad was hurt."

He could almost feel sorry for her when she looked at him, confused. Randal asked her to please take the kids inside and he'd find out what was going on, explaining to her it might have been a mistake all along.

"Oh, of course. They might have gotten the wrong person. I'll just see to them, you go and straighten it out. I do wish you'd reconsider taking over here, Mr. Calhoun. I do. My retirement would go so much better if I knew that the school and the children were in good hands." He told her they'd talk later as he made his way toward his room with her. "He's in my office, just so you know. I wonder how they'd mess up the name like that. Could be causing someone a lot of grief."

"Yes, they might well be." As he made his way to the offices, he told his family what was going on. Or what he thought was going on. Joe told him to wait while Chloe asked him to go in and talk to the man.

He won't be able to get you out to his car unless you let him, right? And there are witnesses in the office too, I'm assuming. Randal said that there wasn't any way, unless he had one of his family. *Everyone is counted for, so that's not it. I'd go in, play along with him, and I'm on my way there. By the way, Randal, are you afraid of guns?*

Hardly. He opened the door to the office and was startled to smell blood in the receptionist area. *I think he's making things a little easier on himself to get me out of here. I think Molly has been hurt.*

If you don't see her, then I would assume that she's dead. Stand in the lobby where I can see you when I come in. He told her he'd try. *Good, that's all we can hope for right now. I'm about a block from you.*

"Hello, Randal. I've come to get you over to the hospital. Your dad and mom have taken a little bit of a tumble. They're going to be all right, but I was sent to get you." He told Chloe what the officer was saying. "Your boss said she'd take care of the kiddies for you."

Chloe told him to engage, but not to leave unless it meant

his life. Randal asked if he could hurt the officer and she told him only if it came to that. Without witnesses, the officer in question could cause a lot of trouble for him...not that he cared, but he said he'd not unless he had no choice.

"You said my mom and dad both are hurt? Do you know what happened?" The officer—no name badge present, so he didn't know what to call him—said that there had been an accident at the mall. "The mall? I didn't know they were headed there today. Thank you for coming to tell me. I'll go on over there—"

"Your brother, he didn't want you to drive." Randal nodded and sat down in the chair usually meant for unruly kids. "If you'd come on with me, we can get there in no time at all. I've got my car right out front."

"I just need a minute." The officer tried to help him up, but Randal knew that he outweighed the guy and that his wolf wasn't happy about being touched. "Just wait. You said that it was just a tumble and they'd be fine. I just need a minute."

"Well, shit." He looked up at the officer when he cursed. "I told him this wasn't gonna work. Get the fuck up."

The gun at his head hurt. Randal had told Chloe he wasn't afraid of them, but that was before he had one pointed at his head. As he stood up, was actually jerked up from the seat, he heard a small popping sound just as the man fell. He looked at Chloe as she stood in the office doorway with her gun out.

She said his name twice before he could focus on what she was saying to him. Randal sat down again and saw the blood begin to pool around the head of the now dead officer. Chloe said his name again.

"You killed him." When he didn't look at her, he felt her fingers dig into his chin and his head jerked around. "He was going to kill me. I think right here in this room. I would have

101

been dead in another few seconds."

"I'm afraid that's true. But you have to focus for me. If you pass out, I'm going to be so fucked. I told your mom that I'd make sure you weren't hurt." Randal wanted to tell her that he didn't need her to be so honest right now, but she moved to the principal's office and came back quickly. "There is a woman in the office back there that has been murdered. She has a name badge of Molly. He killed her to get you out of here in the event that you didn't play nicely with him."

"Why?" Chloe only shrugged. "You've been telling me the truth since you got here, don't stop now. Why was he going to take me? And why me?"

"You are the most trusting of the Calhoun men. You're a teacher of small children that would do anything to keep them safe, including go with a man you don't know with a gun to your head." Randal didn't like that he was pegged and told her that. "I don't either. It means that they've done their homework and knew, I'm sorry to say, that you were the weakest link in the family next to the women. Next time, and there will be a next time, they'll go after the next weakest of them. More than likely Noelle."

"Because she is breeding." He said that they'd not know that unless they had been following her. "Then why her?"

"She doesn't carry a gun. Doesn't seem to have any kind of violent nature to her. And she comes and goes pretty much as she pleases. Elijah is working full time, and she is left alone for the greater part of the day. Not that family isn't close, but she doesn't have someone with her at all times. Sterl is around her, but he usually leaves her alone to run errands as well as pick up furniture that the two of them bought. All they'd have to do is pretend that they have a piece to sell, lure Sterl away, and bam, she's alone again. At a time they can control."

Randal looked at the dead man again. "He would have gotten you to call the house, tell us to come for you in exchange for something he wants—not necessarily what they need, but something—and then he would have blown a hole in your head as soon as you hung up."

"What's the difference between what they want and not what they need?" When she didn't answer him, he looked at her. "Please tell me. I'm terrified that the next time you won't be so close to save my ass."

"What they need is for everyone to back off. Me for looking into the death of my dad. Your grandfather in getting them out of the building." He asked her how that would work if they knew who they were. "Criminals, for the most part, are stupid. Not that a lot of them don't have college educations, or for that matter a good sense of what needs to be done when. But after a time, when they're not caught at whatever it is that they're doing, they get cocky. That is when they make mistakes. I would imagine that William thinks since no one has questioned him on the disappearance of his wife that he's pretty much free and clear of that murder. And his son too. Except for me. I'm not sure that either of them know that I'm looking. If they did, I'd have been killed a long time ago."

"So this, it was for the building. And their plans to keep my grandda out of there." She nodded at him. "So what do we do now? I mean, so far as they know, this guy has gotten me, taken me to wherever, and is making me play ball." He heard the sirens and looked at her again and asked her what she was going to do.

"First of all, you cannot say anything about me. You're going to say that you came in here and found this man dead, along with the woman in the other room. The principal will say that when she left, both the man and the secretary were alive. You'll have no gun residue on your hands, so that will rule you out." He asked her if she trusted the police. "Nope, but by the time they're ready to charge you, which they will, my buddy will be here. You just have to sit tight and tell them you know nothing. Just keep saying you don't know a thing until help arrives."

"Your buddy the Fed." She nodded. "And how will I know who he is? And is he trustworthy?" She was laughing when she moved from where he was through the doorway and out into the hall. As she made her way out, he asked her again. "Chloe? How will I know who he is?"

The police came in with their guns drawn seconds later. He was ordered to stay put, then told to get down on his knees. And through it all, he kept saying he didn't know what had happened.

Everything went according to Chloe's plan, right up to and including him being charged. No one seemed to care that Molly was murdered, but they were upset that one of their own had been shot and killed. And worst yet, that Randal had no idea what had happened to him. His parents and grandparents were saying they'd meet him at the jail just as a very beautiful woman showed up. She winked at him, and he knew in that moment that this was why Chloe was laughing when she left him there. It wasn't a man at all, but a woman.

"My name is Anastasia Sexton, agent for the Federal Bureau of Investigation. I'll be taking over the investigation of this crime." The chief of police, a fat sloppy man named Bob Miles, pushed his way to the woman and demanded to know who she was. "I just told you. Anastasia Sexton. Do you need me to write it down for you to look over later? And, as I said, I'm with the Federal Bureau of Investigation. You've heard of them, haven't you? We're the big boys, in the event you didn't get that part too."

Randal had to hide a smile. Anastasia was speaking slowly for the police, like she thought them simpletons. Which, Randal thought, they were. When Bob said he was in charge, she just walked by him and asked Randal if he was all right.

"I am now. I thought for sure I was going to jail." She winked at him again and told him that Chloe had his back. "You're her friend. She said you were coming. I'm ashamed to say I thought it was a man coming."

"I get that a lot, sadly. Yes, we're friends. And have been for a long time." He figured that would be all he got from her, and was surprised when she smiled at him. "She saved my ass more times than I could tell you about. Not just out in the open forum, but also literally saved my ass."

"Chloe is a good person, and she saved me from being shot on sight today, I think. She's going to marry my brother, Scott." Anastasia nodded, but said nothing as Bob and his men came to where they were standing. "What are you, anyway? Not human, so that'll help. Because I think Bob and his men...I think they mean to run you off. I'm assuming that you know that they're not on the up and up."

"Yeah, he can try. But I have a mouth on me that will scare off a drunken sailor on leave. You just stand back. He might get too mouthy and I'll have to put him down." She looked at him. "That's what you do to mad animals, don't you? Shoot them in the head?" Before he could agree or disagree with her, Bob shoved his large body between them and started talking.

"I want to know by whose authority you have to come in here, into my district, and think to take over a crime against one of my own men. This man here, he's going to my jail, and he's going to answer my questions. You hear me, girly?" Anastasia just stood there and said nothing. "Now, I'm glad

105

you are seeing things my way, and if you'll just move that pretty little body of yours out of the way, we'll take him in. Go on now, you just go on over there and stay out of the way of my men."

Randal was standing right next to her when she moved. He'd been looking at Bob and his men when it happened. He was pretty sure that even if he'd had a camera out, recording every second of the last few minutes, he would have missed it. Covering his mouth so it wouldn't be hanging open, he surveyed the little office.

Bob was pressed against the wall with his arm jerked up behind his back, while his men, all three of them, were down on the floor, curled up and holding their cocks like they'd been kicked hard, as well as nursing their other wounds. One of them, Randal could see, had a broken arm. Another of them was bleeding from his nose and mouth. Randal looked at Bob, who was screaming his head off about being in pain. He supposed he was, the way Anastasia was holding him there.

"Shut up." The compulsion was there; he'd never felt it so strong before, and felt his own mouth snap closed. When Anastasia asked him to call an ambulance, he pulled out his phone while she continued to talk to Bob. "What part of 'I'm taking over this crime scene' did you not understand? I was pretty sure that I'd made that perfectly clear. I even went so far as to tell you that I was with the FBI and that I was one of the big boys. By the way, that was pretty sexiest calling me a girly. I might have to bring you up on charges of sexual harassment. That is, if you survive this. Then you had to go all show-boaty and come over here and act like a big man. You know what, I've had bigger turds flushed down my toilet than you. Now, we're going to do this again. I'm taking over the investigation of this crime. Do you have a problem with that?"

"Yes, you mother fucking, cunt, I have a—" The scream coming from Bob was loud enough to make glass rattle and his ears hurt. Bob was sobbing now, big fat tears rolling down his cheeks as he threatened Anastasia again. "You're going to pay for that bitch, see if you don't. I'm the law around here, and I'll say when you're going to—"

There was no scream this time, only the thud of Bob hitting the floor. Randal had no idea what she'd done to the cop other than dislocate his arm and shoulder, but since he was still breathing and his heart was still beating, he didn't care.

Others were showing up now, their guns drawn as they surrounded the building. He was afraid now, not for him, but the others in the building. Reinforcements meant more idiots to fire at him. When he thought about the children in the rooms, he turned to Anastasia and asked her what was going to happen.

"They won't be harmed, none of them will. I've had a few people take them out the back of the building and to safety. Now it's your turn. Randal, it's time you left before someone gets seriously hurt." He nodded and moved to the hall and to the back of the school. When Anastasia said his name, he turned back to her. "I'm fae. And please tell Chloe that I'll see her soon."

~~~

Scott was still trying to wrap his head around the fact that Randal had nearly been kidnapped and then killed. By the police. In his school. Scott looked at Elijah when he sat down next to him. His family had been doing that for the past few hours. Coming to just sit by him. But he had a feeling that Elijah had something to say.

107

KATHI S. BARTON

"I'm to tell you.... No, that's not right. I'm to inform you that should you like to talk to your mate, you'd better do it now." Scott asked him why. "I think she has it in her head that she's going after the Flynns. Alone."

"No. I talked to her. She said she'd back off and let the professionals handle it." Elijah asked him when that had been. "This morning. Before all this shit when down. Why?"

"I think she's changed her mind since then." Elijah nodded to the group standing by the front door. "Did you know that she has friends in very high places? And that these friends all seem to think that they owe her in some way?"

"Randal said that the agent that is taking over the police department is fae, and that she would see Chloe later. He told me that she said Chloe had saved her ass a few times. I wonder what she did." Elijah said that he'd met her too and that he didn't know. "I'm in over my head here."

"You think? Why is that?" Scott looked at the nine people that had shown up at his house about two hours ago. "Them? I think they're here to help with this crap, not get in your way."

"It's not just that. I think that I can't protect her like I want to. Or how I should. If anything, I think she's the one that's going to be doing the protecting. I never would have thought that from the beginning of this. But damn, she's good." Elijah just laughed. "I don't think this is the least bit funny."

"I do. Christ man, do you think that Trent thinks he's in over his head?" They looked at their older brother now. He seemed to be enjoying all the hoopla that was going on around him. "Joe could and has easily taken care of him for months now. She has more money than he does, or ever thought to have. They have a vampire living in their sub levels that doesn't seem to want anything from them but friendship. And she's much stronger than Trent will ever be on his best days.

Yet there he sits, acting like he's got a handle on everything. And then look at me. Noelle has no special powers, not really, but what she does have is me wrapped up around her little finger. I can and do protect her, but she takes care of me in ways that no one will ever be able to understand. I'm calmed by her. I feel better than I have in decades simply because she loves me. And I'm going to be a father. You have no idea how that can make a man feel until you know that someone you created is going to call you Dad."

Scott knew all this. Hell, he'd been thinking of all kinds of ways that he could stay out of her way when she was working. And she was working too. But in a way that you'd not notice unless you were paying attention. Like just a bit ago.

Anastasia had wanted to appoint one of the officers that didn't seem to have any kind of ties to the things going on in the stationhouse. Chloe had simply pulled up his bank records, and they could see that very large sums of money had been hitting his account on the tenth of each month, then disappearing the required twenty-four hours later. When the bank was called, they said that not only had the man in question set it up to go overseas, but he'd made sure that his wife hadn't been on the signature card. That in all their books made him a bad cop. Someone somewhere was paying him off, and he wasn't sharing with his family.

Then there had been the peek into Bob's house. Noah had done that for them, simply because Chloe had mentioned that Bob might have something there that would help them figure out who was to be trusted. Not only had they found out that *all* the men and women that worked there were on someone's payroll, but that a lot of them had criminal records when their real names were looked into. When Chloe joined him on the couch, he picked her up and sat her on his lap.

"Thank you. I think I needed you to hold me for a bit." He told her he needed it as well. "I just found out that George has hired a hitman to take out his father."

"I'm sorry, what?" She told him what she'd been able to find out so far. "So, he's going to have his dad killed because he thinks he is going to be rich? Do you suppose he knows that his dad buried his wife in the basement of the business he works at? And perhaps someone else?"

"No, I don't know why but I don't think so. I think if he had known, he'd be blackmailing his dad. I have your brother Tanner looking into finding out who his mom might be. If she's alive, then she might be able to shed some light on a few things." He asked her what. "Well, for one thing, how did William end up with his son? And why did she have a relationship with William when it's obvious that it didn't go all that far? I'm assuming for now that she's out there, but I doubt it."

"Why is that important?" Chloe told him that maybe the girlfriend knew about the death of the wife. "You think so?"

"No, not really. I think, like her son, if she had known she'd more than likely either be in the big house with him or he'd be paying her off to keep her quiet. I can't see that happening. They're too broke, for one thing, and if she was out there, which I'm doubting, then she'd be coming around when he stopped paying her, if he ever did." Scott held her, thinking of how her mind worked. "You think I'm nuts."

"No, I think you're brilliant. I would have just assumed that she was out there and didn't care. But you put a spin on it that makes me believe that this Flynn guy is scarier than we thought. Not only has he killed a few people, but he's covered up a few murders too. He seems to be going to great links to keep us out of the building as well, so I think once we get in there, it's going to fall apart for him. Too bad we can't just go there and dig up the floor anyway." She sat up suddenly. "What did I say?"

"It's a rental." He nodded. "According to the law, the owner of the property can go in and inspect it at any time."

"Yeah, so?" Scott wasn't getting it, but he loved seeing her so excited. "Grandda wouldn't know what to look for if he was to go in, and I'm pretty sure that you'd have to have some kind of clue to dig up a basement floor, right? And to be honest, even as a wolf, I'd not feel good about him going in there alone."

"He won't have to be alone. He can take in anyone that he wants to help him look around." She jumped up off his lap and did a little dance. He laughed so hard, he nearly missed what she said. "I'm going to get to go in there and mess things up."

"Mess what up? And you're not going in there alone. Not if I can help you." But she was going to the others still huddled together. When one of the people standing there yelled "hot damn" he figured that whatever the plan was, it was going to be executed.

Standing up, he went to find his grandda. "I want you to sell me the building that you're renting to the Flynn's. I'll sell it back to you, but for now, I'd like to buy it from you."

"Why?" He told him what Chloe had told him. "All right. I can see that you'd want to be there with her. I'll sell it to you for a buck. And when you guys have finished up with this mess, I'll buy it back if I want it still, and we'll have a party when we tear it down. Because as of the moment we find that poor woman's body down there, I don't want to have another thing to do with it. You know that just ain't right."

"Yes, and I'm sorry, Grandda. There are all sorts of

monsters around. But as for the building, it's a deal." He handed his grandda the dollar and they went to find someone to notarize the sale. Other than the filing, which would be done in the morning, he now owned the Flynn Computers building. And he was going to help his mate take down a couple of bastards.

He just hoped she thought what he'd done was a good idea too. Scott was afraid that pissing off his mate could have dire consequences. She was sort of mean when she wanted to be. He thought of ways to tie her down to talk to her, and had to adjust his cock. Yes, sir, he thought he was going to make sure that she couldn't hurt him when he talked to her.

Chapter 8

Chloe wasn't afraid of what was going to happen to her, but she was a little nervous. Some of the equipment that they'd put together had some very strange uses. All of which Scott, or Master now, was going to show her. Not tonight, but he was going to show her some. Chloe looked down at the outfit that she'd been told to put on.

"Are you okay with this?" Smiling at him, she said that she was. "Now, as soon as you're ready, we can begin. I don't want you to feel rushed or anything, so when it's too much, just say ginger. I want this to be as much fun for you as it is for me. But like I said, if it's not your thing or you don't like it, we'll stop."

"I'm not afraid." He nodded, still looking unsure. "Do you give your clients this much help when you help them out?"

"Yes. Sometimes. It's sort of a test, to see how much they really want to be a part of this lifestyle. There are people who read about it and think that it's for them, when in reality, it's not. It's either too violent for them, which it can be on some levels, or they are in the wrong position." She asked him what he meant. "There have been times when a couple will come to me for help, and all their problem turns out to be is that they needed to switch roles. The woman be the Dom and the other half be the sub."

She wasn't sure she wanted to be in charge of anything that might go on in here. Looking around, she saw herself in the mirror behind her. Walking to it, careful of her shoes, she looked at Scott when he came up behind her. When he looked at her like he was now, she felt sexy, desirable. Loved.

"This suits you. I wasn't sure, but it really does." Her body was wrapped in leather. Dark strips of the softest material outlined her breasts and hips. Her pussy was uncovered too, in a way that made her feel both exposed and sexy. There was a blindfold on her head, just waiting for him to tell her it was time to start. The shoes she had on were leather strips as well. The soles of them were high heeled, yet still soft around her feet. She didn't wear heels much and was afraid of falling over. Whatever he was going to do to her, Chloe was excited for it.

"I thought there would be a collar for some reason." He told her that she'd not earned it as yet. "I'll work hard in getting that then."

"I know you will. Are you ready?" She stepped back from him now and looked at what he wore. "What do you think?"

He had on a pair of tight leather pants that matched her own outfit. A Velcro front held them around him, and would uncover his cock when he was ready, he'd told her. No shirt, and he had a small riding crop in his hand. She felt her pussy soak when she thought of the things he might do to her with that.

When he told her to get on her knees, she panicked just a little when the blindfold was put over her eyes. But as soon as he touched her face below it, she calmed a great deal. This was a trial run; she knew this, but she wanted to make sure that he didn't regret bringing her into his lifestyle.

"Suck my cock." Putting out her hands to find him, she felt the sting of the whip. "I didn't say you could touch me with your hands. I ordered you to suck my cock."

He snapped it against her skin again, and instead of being pissed about it, she felt her body warm to the pain. When his cock touched her lips, she opened her mouth to take him.

It took her several seconds to get used to sucking him like this. Not being able to touch him or herself, she moved her head over him. When he moaned once, she knew that at least on some level she was doing it right. And when she swallowed around him, bringing him past the tight muscles in her throat, she nearly came when he touched the whip to her backside again.

"I'm not going to come this way." He didn't sound so sure about that, she thought, and swallowed again. "Christ, you're killing me."

Again and again she pleasured him. It was too much and not enough at the same time. The need, the desire to give herself relief was nearly too overwhelming, and she had to dig her nails into her palms not to touch either of them. Shifting slightly on her knees gave her some relief, but it also caused her to want more. Then he was gone.

She wanted to take off the blindfold, to see how she had affected him. But she didn't move, not even to shift off her knees that were starting to hurt a little. When Scott told her to stand up, she wasn't sure how steady she was going to be and nearly reached out for something to hold on to. But as soon as she stood on her own, Chloe felt like she'd accomplished a milestone.

Something soft touched her ass. Not moving, she tried to figure out what it was. And when something lashed painfully over her nipples, she cried out only to be slapped again and again for making a noise.

"Do you want me to stop?" Shaking her head, she told him no. "Say it, slave, say your safe word and we'll stop now."

"I'm not going to stop, Master." Her body burned now from the way the pain in her nipples seemed to touch every part of her. It was a wonderful kind of pain, something that she wanted a good deal more of.

"Don't move." She didn't acknowledge his command but stood still. Then when his mouth suckled on her bruised and sore nipple, she wanted to beg him to fuck her, to take her now. Then the incredible pain of something being pinched on her made her cry out. "It's a nipple clamp. I'm only going to give you one of them today. And not for very long. Once you can tolerate them, or decide you don't like them, we can work from there."

She wasn't sure already. It was painfully tight, and her breast felt like it was being ripped from her body. But then she felt a breath of air float over her, his warm scent seeming to engulf her in love and a hazy kind of drug.

Chloe was moved then, to some kind of metal bar that had her arms pulled above her head. Still not sure she enjoyed the thing at her breast, she tried her best not to cry out when his fingers brushed over it. Then the pain was gone, and in its place was the most wonderful feeling of relief. Scott blew over her again and this time she came.

"I should beat you for that." She didn't care if he beat her until she couldn't walk. Her body was still humming from coming like she had. "If I tell you that you'll never come that hard again, will you believe me?"

116

"Yes." He laughed and told her that she would, double what she'd just experienced. "I don't think I'll survive that."

"I don't think either of us will." When her arms were pulled up a little higher, she moved her legs where he pulled them. The straps at her ankles didn't feel heavy, but they were tight. When he told her not to move again, she knew her heartrate had doubled.

His fingers brushed over her in different places. Her breasts, her hip. Then her toes. When he touched his mouth to the back of her knee, she wanted to moan, needed to as a matter of fact. But before she could beg for more, more of it all, he was gone again and something harder, firmer touched her in the same places.

"When I have you here, I'll expect no less from you than before. You'll do as I tell you when I tell you without question." She wasn't sure if she was supposed to answer, so didn't. "And when I want to fuck you, you'll take it. Even if you don't get the pleasure of my cum."

So long as she could come, she'd be all right, Chloe told herself. Her arms were massaged, her breasts suckled. Each time he touched her, she could feel his cock touching her, brushing slightly over her heated flesh. His mouth touched her hip this time, his tongue played with her navel. By the time he touched her from behind, his cock at her ass, she could have easily begged him to beat her so that she could come again.

"I'm going to eat you like this. Spread out before me like a feast. And you're not to come." She nearly told him that wasn't fair, that she needed it badly, when he spoke again. "If you manage not to come until I tell you, I will reward you greatly, slave."

Game on, she thought to herself. She'd not come now

117

even if she had to bite through her lips to keep from doing it. There were noises now, small little sounds that should have been easy for her to focus on, but she couldn't. It sounded like a door had opened and closed. For a few moments she thought he'd left her there, then his hands were on her ass, his mouth kissing the area just above her pussy.

The click of a switch startled her. Scott spread her nether lips; she felt the coolness of the air on her and tried to shy away from it. Then something touched her, vibrated against her so gently that she rocked into it.

"You aren't to come." Nodding, she felt his mouth at her pussy, his fingers digging into her flesh. And when he suckled her into his mouth and bit down, Chloe bit down on her tongue. Christ, he was trying to kill her.

Over and over he tortured her this way. The vibrator would touch her, bringing her the most incredible pleasure, then was taken away. His mouth would bite her pussy, her hips, or her thigh, and Chloe would feel like she was being set afire, her entire body hot from need.

Every time she was close, ready to say fuck it all and just come, he would tell her that she only had to release. That she could end this by saying her safe word. It made her all the more determined to win this war. And that was what it had become, a war.

Finally, he stopped. Nothing moved, no more touches to her skin. The vibrator was gone too. As she stood there, her body drenched in sweat, she waited for his next move, not sure what it would be, but she was going to win. The blindfold was jerked from her face and she looked up at Scott.

"His turn."

~~~

Scott let his wolf take him. It was that or he was going to

beg her to let him fuck her. She was killing him, her ability to be his slave well beyond anything he could have imagined. Or had hoped for. Chloe was his sub, his mate for all time, and he was going to enjoy training her to be his partner as well.

His wolf lunged at her. Lapping at her pussy, he could tell that he wanted more, he needed to take her to new heights. His teeth sank into her thigh, her calf, and pussy. He ate her like a fine steak, a last meal and the best dessert of all time. Scott let him have her, all of her he wanted, and so did Chloe. And when he backed off, giving him back his body, Scott stood up and took her mouth as he slammed his cock deep into her pussy.

"Come." She screamed out his name as he fucked her hard. Every time she came, tightening her sheath around his cock, he felt his need compound, his cock ache just a little more. And when she came a third time, he gave her his throat, told her to bite him to draw blood. As soon as she did, bit him harder than he'd thought she would, Scott came. He filled her with his seed so many times that he lost count.

When he could no longer move, barely able to stand on his own two feet, he held onto her. Scott knew that she was hurting, the bars weren't made for that much activity, but he couldn't stand yet and wasn't sure he'd be able to help her down. Lifting his head, he looked down at her and saw tears on her cheeks.

"I'm so sorry." She shook her head and his own heart crumbled. He knew that she'd not enjoyed herself like he thought she had. Scott reached up to unlatch her hands from the bar. "We can leave here and not return."

"If you do that I'm going to find my gun and shoot you." He looked at her again. "I have never in all my life come that many times and that hard. Christ, Scott, I thought for sure that

119

when I came that first time I was done, but you gave me so much more. Sex has always meant nothing to me. Now, with you, it's my world."

"I thought you hated it." When her arm was free, he helped her massage the feelings back into it. "You were crying. I thought you didn't enjoy yourself."

"Are you kidding? I was crying because it was so wonderful. And I discovered that I love you." He paused in working the other hand loose from the bar. Scott asked her what she'd said. "I said that I love you. With all my heart."

"Oh, Chloe, I love you as well. With all that I am." He got her free from the arm bars and held her to him. "Chloe, you really did enjoy this? I mean, it's all right if you didn't."

"This was the most mind blowing sex I've never had, and please don't take it from me." He laughed; he just couldn't help it, he was so happy. "I don't know if I could do this every night, but I would love to come in here often."

"No, not every night." He kissed her then, gave her all that he could in it. When he lifted his head again, Scott held her to his body and realized that he hadn't felt this good in all his life. And all because of Chloe.

They took a shower together. He couldn't seem to stop touching her and she him. As he washed her hair, he marveled at the way the soap bubbles moved over her flesh, the way that the water chasing them was sexy.

They ended up making love again, this time gently without whips or clips. And when he turned the water off, he reached for a warm towel and laughed when she yawned as many times as he did.

Drying her body, working out the soreness that he knew would be there in the morning, he talked to her. Not of anything important or of the things that were going on around them, but of his childhood. Growing up with five brothers and having his parents and grandparents around all the time.

"One Christmas my grandparents showed up without telling anyone they were coming home. I think that was the year that we managed to both break my mom's heart and give her the best Christmas ever." She asked him what they'd done. "We were thinking we were too old for Christmas. I know that sounds really lame, but Tanner had just gotten his driver's license and we were all out in the working world for the most part and we didn't want a tree. Trent had come up with the idea that we should all get money instead of getting gifts from our parents."

"Oh Scott, you didn't. My dad and I exchanged gifts right up until he died. It was the best time finding things for him and wrapping them up." He told her he'd almost figured that out too late. "So how did you idiots turn it around?"

"Grandma. She came into the house that was devoid of even a tree and huffed at us. Then she sat us down in the living room and told us how disappointed she was in us all." Scott remembered the pain of disappointing any of them, but especially his mom and grandma. "She went on to tell us how our mom had spent the entire year, from the day after Christmas to the day before, picking out the perfect gifts for us. Finding a wrapping paper that held special meaning to her. How, even though she didn't cook a lick, she had found things for us to enjoy that would bring happiness to her home. And we had in one swift move taken it all from her."

"Then what did she do? I hope she beat all your asses. I would have if I had been her." Scott told her that what Grandma had done was far worse. "Good for her."

"She told us that someday that there would be no grandmas or grandpas around. That our parents would pass

121

on as well. Then she asked us, what sort of memories will you take to your heart? Ones that had us getting a stark envelope with cash in it, or a memory of sitting around the tree as a family, opening not just beautiful gifts, but fun ones as well." He had hurt then when she'd pointed out that they'd not be around forever, and did now as well. "Then she told us to get our asses in gear and get to Christmas. None of us grumbled how it was two days before the big event, but got into our cars and drove to the mall in a snowstorm. I think we had the best time that year, all of us working together to get presents for everyone. And when we got home, the house was bright with lights and the tree was up. It was as if it was only waiting for us to get our heads out of our asses before it shone."

"What a wonderful story. I knew that I liked your grandma. I think I might even love her a little more because she took you all to task. But she does sort of scare me a bit." Scott laughed and asked her why. "Because I'm not sure if you've noticed this or not, but she rules this place. Your mom does most of the time, but the moment your grandma shows up, the house changes. Like it was well run before, but almost military like after she shows up."

"I'm not going to tell her what you said. If she thinks she's in charge, then it might go to her head." He sobered up a little when he thought what had happened to them after that. "The next year my grandda on my mom's side passed away. He just went to bed and didn't get up. Three months later, Grandma went with him. She said she wasn't meant to be without him, and simply let herself die too."

"And now we're all immortals." He nodded as they were turning off lights to head up to their bed. "Joe told me that you all received magic when she became Trent's mate. Is this something I should know about? I mean, I got some of it, I

122

guess. But I don't know what."

"You can change with a thought. I mean, your clothing." He showed her how to do it, and smiled when she put on a very sexy nighty. "Yes, I love the way your mind works. Also, before we get too far into discovering how many things you can change into, you can read peoples' minds. I already could, but it's something that you have to practice at."

"What happens if I don't practice?" He explained that it was not what happens so much as what she could do to hurt someone. "That's what it means to be mind raped then."

"Pretty much." She changed into a pair of soft terry pants and a tee shirt, and he knew there was something she was going to tell him. Scott wasn't ready for it. No matter what it might be. "Will you marry me?"

"Yes. But I have to tell you something first." He wasn't sure she heard him correctly, so he repeated his question. "I said yes. I would love to marry you. But I really have to tell you this. It's about Anastasia."

"Is it bad news?" She told him no. "Then can it wait until later? I'm exhausted and I'm sure you are as well. Just tell me in the morning, if it can wait."

"I suppose it can." They climbed into the big bed and he pulled her body to his. He could get used to this, having her close all the time. "Scott, I love you."

"And I love you." He held her, his mind going a mile a minute on how he was going to make her the happiest woman in the world. He was going to start by taking her on the trip she'd been planning, then he was going to change her. If she wanted. To have her as his mate and wolf...Scott knew they'd be running the woods for days at a time.

He felt the touch seconds before Noah spoke. The vampire and he had exchanged blood a few weeks ago. Scott wasn't sure why Noah had thought that they should, but he'd said it would all be revealed. Scott just liked having the man around. He was a good friend.

I was just speaking to Joe. I am to understand that you have purchased the building from your grandfather so that you might go into the building with the inspector. Scott told him that was right. *I was wondering if you were aware that you normally must give at least twenty-four hour notice to enter the premises. But as the new owner, you don't have to do that. You need only to say that you're inspecting it for insurance purposes.*

You're sure about that? Noah said that he was reasonably sure, but he could ask someone. *No, I think you might be right. We were worried that if we gave them enough notice that they'd skip town.*

I would imagine that they would. They aren't the best of people. Also, I wanted to let you know that the young wife is dead. Her body will be discovered in a few hours by an unknown tipster. Scott thanked him. *Sadly, it wasn't me. Your new friend the fae has connections that I can never hope to get. She simply asked the earth for help and she got it. I'd look into what sort of fae she is if I were you.*

There are different kinds? Noah told him there were as many fae as there were snowflakes. Each of them different in some way. *That is a scary amount of magic.*

It is. She is...I have heard that she is quite the beauty. However, I think to avoid her myself. I should very much like a little taste of her, but I think she'd cause me a great deal of harm. Scott told Noah that he might find that she was really nice. *Yes, but I am a vampire and she is...well, she is fae. We are mortal enemies, her kind and I. I'm very old, very powerful, but I think she will top me should it come to that. Nah, my friend, I will try hard to avoid her.*

After talking about plans to meet up soon, the connection

was closed. Scott felt better now; he was going to be able to get things going sooner than they thought. Closing his eyes, he thought of all the work that needed to be done on the house, and decided that he'd work hard to get it completed. Christmas was coming soon, and he wanted to have his house ready for the holidays.

Chapter 9

George was just leaning back in his chair when someone knocked. This was going to ruin his nice buzz, he just knew it. So telling the person to go away, he was on the phone, he closed his eyes just as the door flew open. There stood Chloe and a man he'd never seen before.

"So have you decided to come back to work for me? I don't know, Chloe, you left here without notice." She told him he had dust on his nose. Wiping it off, he felt his temper take a nasty turn. "Listen bitch. I told you to go away. If you see something that you don't like, it's all your fault. Go the fuck away."

"I'm here with the new owner. And he wants to make a thorough inspection of the place." He asked her if his dad had gotten the place finally. "No, dumbass, he's never going to get this place."

"Well, then, I'm telling you that you can't come in." She just looked around and he realized that she was already there. "What I mean is, you're not doing anything without my dad here."

"That's what we're hoping for." He didn't understand that but reached for the phone. He was sort of hoping that she'd tell him they'd come back some other time; he wasn't keen on calling his dad right now. "Call him, George. We have better things to do than to wait all day for you to make a decision."

His dad was really pissed at him. Yesterday he'd not come to the computer store at all, which meant that it hadn't been unlocked for anyone to go inside. He didn't understand what the big deal was. They never had any customers coming in now anyway.

"Because, as I have told you several times before, if we don't keep the appearances of having a business there, then that fucking bastard Calhoun can close us down. I've mentioned to you before how important it is that he doesn't close us down, haven't I?" He had, but George still didn't get it. "If you can't be bothered to go to work, then I will find someone that will. And pay them for the shitty job that you're not doing."

So here he was, snorting his last stuff until he could find his friend and dealer. Hopefully someone would come in and need some work done so he'd have the cash to pay him without digging into his briefcase. He had often wondered if he could sell off the shit here for the cash and let his dad think he was working. George didn't think anything here was worth much anyway. Not even the building.

The place was a dump, and there was something going on with the electric too. It kept blinking out when he turned on his coffee pot and cooked his snacks in the zapper. The bathroom stopped up a lot, the doors were all loopy and didn't close well. And the air only worked sometimes. He looked at Chloe when she said his name. He'd completely forgotten about her.

"Call your dad, George, so we can get this over with. Tell

him that we're starting without him too." George nodded and picked up the phone. There was no hope for it, his dad was going to be pissed.

"Chloe is here. She said that she's come with the new owners. I didn't know the place was for sale." His dad cursed long and loud. "I'm guessing by your anger that you didn't know it was either."

"What the fuck is she doing there now? Ask her." George already knew that and told his dad. "What do you mean, they're there to inspect the place? They can't do that without notice. Tell her she has to get the fuck out of there now."

Before he could relay the message to her, she laid a paper down in front of him. He read it over twice before he had to tell his dad. And that didn't improve his mood one bit.

"There is no such law." George told his dad he was looking right at it. She'd been kind enough to print it out for him. "Bull shit. You tell her that I'm on my way and that she'd better not touch a fucking thing."

The phone slammed down in his ear and George sat there. Chloe and the man were already starting, going through the office next to his. George looked around his own office and tried to think what might be there that would get him into trouble. He'd brought his briefcase in just this morning, having finally given permission to the staff at home to clean his room.

George had no idea what had gone wrong with his dump he'd taken on his dirty laundry, but it had gotten all over his carpet and his bed before he'd had to find help. His room was cleared of things that he didn't want the staff to find, but most of it was here now. And he was pretty sure that it was more than he wanted to get caught with. Especially all the cash.

Standing up, he took out his gun and put it in his pants

pocket. Picking up his briefcase, he was out the door and into the parking lot even before he thought of what he was doing. Getting into his car, he tried to think. His head was buzzing too much for him to keep all his thoughts in any kind of order, so he started his car and sat there. He looked in his case only to find that he'd left some very key things in the building.

"I left my notes." He started to laugh, suddenly finding everything to be just hilarious. "Dad is not going to be happy when he finds out my plan."

The notes were his plans for not just what he wanted to say when he was informed that his dad was dead, but the payment plan that he'd set up to pay off his killer. He knew that paying a man that killed for a living was important. George did not want to end up on the wrong end of his gun. Then there was the insurance policy that he'd taken out on his dad, as well as the unpaid bills that he'd taken to carrying around with him so no one would be the wiser. His dad might hire someone to kill him when he found them. He wouldn't put it past his dad to do something like that.

There were also his written out thoughts on the night that his dad had come into his room. His diary was there. It was the one that he'd been given when he'd stayed at the last clinic, and had his thoughts as well as things he'd done since he'd been let out. He thought of the day his dad had come to him, telling him that he'd killed Mike Davis.

George had written down as much as he could remember that was said that night, but he knew there were things missing. He also wrote out how his dad had seemed manic, maybe even a little drunk as well.

His dad had told George that he'd just killed a cop. At first he'd thought his dad was saying that he himself had done it, that he'd been the one driving the car. But he'd been blaming

George for it. Telling him that in a drunken state, he'd hit a cop and killed him. And no matter how many times George told him that he'd been there all night, his dad had insisted that he'd just gotten home.

"Do you have any idea what this is going to cost me if it gets out? How much damage control I'm going to have to do to get you out of this?" George begged his father to tell him he'd fix this. Even though he had no idea when or how it had happened. He'd been too stoned, he'd told him, to even leave the house. Or so he'd thought. "You were out, damn it. I know you were. How else was the car you were driving damaged and covered in blood?"

"But I didn't do a damned thing, Dad." That had earned him a slap to the face, and then his dad had hit him over and over until George had to run. He'd left with his gun that he had now and nothing else. Not even a credit card or cash. It had taken two days for his dad to let him back in the house, and since then, George had been careful never to drive again, not unless he had to.

The very next day after he was home it was all over the news that Officer Davis had been killed and that it looked like a case of hit and run. George watched every news report for a week after, even going to far as to record them so he could make sure his name was never mentioned. Then the other morning, he'd found the note.

"I didn't do it." His dad had paid off a man by the name of Casey. There was a bank note for it, and in the memo part it had accident. There was blood on the note, along with instructions that when he got rid of the car and wiped it down, he was to return for the rest of the money. He knew his dad well enough to know that had George killed a cop, he would have let him hang for it. George knew then that not only had his dad done

131

it, but he had paid to have the car destroyed as well.

As he sat there he thought of all kinds of things that his dad had blamed him for. The disappearance of his mom was just one of many things over the years. There was also this woman that he had no idea who she was, but his dad had told George he'd killed her. He even showed George the pictures of her dead body. It had sickened him, now even more so since he knew that his dad had done it. Done it all.

He knew that Cybil wasn't his real mother; hell, he'd been almost her age when she married up with his dad. Only five or so years had been the difference, but she was much smarter than he knew he'd ever be. She made sure he knew that he was a child of an affair. That he'd never amount to anything because his mom was a whore. No amount of trying to prove himself to her, that he could be better, would change her mind. He supposed that he'd not tried all that hard, but she still shouldn't have left the way she had.

When his cell phone started to chirp, a ringtone that he knew was his dad's, George laid the phone on the other seat. Whatever his dad was going to say to him, he didn't want to hear it. It was more than likely something else that he'd done wrong. George watched as a cruiser flew past his parking spot. No doubt his dad sending in the police to make sure that Chloe was stopped. He doubted very much it would stop her. Chloe was pretty determined. He'd noticed that right away.

George had had to hire her. His dad had told him it was his penance for killing her father. George hadn't pointed out, yet again, that he'd not done it, but he'd hired her all the same. She was a good worker and was kind to the people that worked there...even him on occasion. George had actually enjoyed going to work at the beginning, knowing that she'd be there. Where he could hear her soft voice. Watch her work with the other employees when they had trouble getting the job done.

Then his dad had told him that she was spying on him. He'd even shown him video of her snooping around the building. Going into areas that had been closed off for years. When she'd been down in the basement, his dad had screamed at him for hours about that, like he could have stopped her if he didn't know what she was doing until that moment.

His phone made a noise signaling that he had a message. It took him several tries to get the password correct, and he had hoped that he'd get locked out and not be able to hear it. But on the third try, he got it open.

George listened to the voice mail that his dad had left him. "There is no hope for it, son. You're going to go to prison. They'll find out soon enough that you killed that man and the others, and you'll go away for a very long time. No dope will be there to keep you company. You should come in now, come here and confess. It's the least you could do after all I've done for you."

George pulled out his gun. His grandma had given it to him so long ago now he could barely remember her face. She'd told him that there might be a time when he'd need to use it. That he was to point it with authority and to pull the trigger like he meant it.

"No pussy footing around, Georgie my boy. You use it like a man." She'd been the only person he'd allowed to call him that. He'd been her Georgie boy, and would be forever, he supposed. He thought of her now and wondered what she might think of him.

"I'm such a failure." He wasn't going to change that fact. He'd been a fuck up since the day he'd been born. Even then, as a kid, he'd known that he wasn't going to amount to anything. His dad had told him that over and over. Cybil had too, in her nasty way. Nor would he ever be loved again. "I wish you were here, Grannie. I really do."

Turning on the radio, he listened for a moment to the man's voice. He had no idea what he was talking about, but found some comfort in his voice. But as he fingered his gun, he knew that no matter what, he was going to go down for the murder of that cop. And he'd not done it. Instead of waiting for the killer to do the job of taking out his dad, George decided that he'd take care of things on his own.

"I should have taken care of it long ago." Turning off the radio, he sat there thinking of his grandma. Point it with authority and pull the trigger like you mean it. Touching his fingers to the gun that had meant so much to him, he nodded once. Picking it up, he turned it over in his hand. Then he put it in his mouth and pulled the trigger.

~~~

Anastasia stood by the door while they looked around. Scott wasn't sure what he was supposed to be looking for, but he did poke around at a couple of boxes that were wet. He wondered if there was a leak, and decided that it wouldn't have surprised him. The place really was falling down around their ears.

"We have to make it look good." Nodding at Chloe, he told her that he wasn't sure how to go about making it look good. "Yeah, this place is nasty."

They heard running feet above them and he wondered what was going on now. Twenty minutes ago William had shown up with his attorney, and he'd been informed that they could indeed go through the building without interference from him. William sure could string a bunch of curse words together, Scott thought with a laugh.

"Guys? You might want to come up here."

Scott could hear the concern in Anastasia's voice, and he was suddenly afraid. They'd done nothing to the basement that would require them to have a crew come in, and he was afraid that they'd failed. As they made their way up the stairs, he could hear sobbing. Then William was cursing. As soon as they entered the room where he was, he launched himself at Chloe. Scott just barely got her out of the way before William could hurt her.

"This is all your fucking fault. You did this."

Scott wasn't sure what was going on and looked at Anastasia for help.

"We found George about five minutes ago. He's dead." Scott looked at William, and before he could ask him why he'd killed his son, she continued. "It looks like a self-inflicted gunshot to the head. We're treating it as a suicide for now, but no one is leaving here until we are sure."

George was dead? He wondered what that would do to their investigation. Then he felt horrible. The man had killed himself, and here he was thinking about his own work. He told William he was sorry for his loss.

"You should be sorry, you mother fucker. This is all your doing. You and that fucking family of yours. He was a good boy and you guy drove him to this." Scott said nothing; there wasn't any point in it, he thought. "I'm going to own your asses for this. See if I don't. And all that I've done in trying to protect him, all my hard work to keep him safe is over."

"What sort of things were you protecting him from? I mean, he was a grown man. Responsible for his own actions." Chloe didn't take her eyes off William, and he wondered what she was up to. "You and him, you guys protected each other, didn't you? I mean, he knew shit about you, you about him.

135

Sort of a partnership, wouldn't you call it?"

"He was my son. I don't know what you're getting at." Chloe just shrugged and started away. "No, you get your skinny ass back here. I want to know what you mean by that. Tell me."

"I'm not sure if you're aware of this, but you are not my boss any longer. Not that you were ever here, but you don't get to tell me what to do and when to do it." She looked over at Scott and smiled. "You can, but he can't. Right?"

"Yes, that's right." He had no idea what she was doing, but he'd play along with her. "In fact, I was thinking that we need to finish up what we were doing before being called away. I'd like to get this inspection over—"

"You'll do no such thing. I want you to get the hell out of my building." Scott pointed out that it was his building. "No, it's mine. I work here and it's mine to do with as I see fit. You'll stop this nonsense right this minute."

Chloe left the room and he followed her. Scott wasn't sure if William would come after them or not, but didn't worry about it. With Anastasia there, he figured she'd keep them safe. As they made their way to the basement again, he was surprised to see his brothers, all of them armed with sledge hammers. He asked them what they were doing.

"In about two minutes, there is going to be a water main break in here." He asked Trent if he was going to make it. "Nah. We all are. It'll be fun. Wait and see."

As soon as the first bit of rock breaking sounded around the room, he heard someone running again. Even before he could tell his brothers to watch out, he heard the gun go off. Scott had turned to slam the door shut to keep them at least slightly safer when Chloe fell into his arms.

"Christ." Trent knocked him back; he looked down at his

mate and saw the blood then. She was covered it in. He looked at Trent when he slapped him. "Did you hear me? I said shift. You have to start the conversion now or she's dead."

His wolf seemed to understand the urgency more than he did and took him. As soon as he was fully wolf, his counterpart threw back his head and howled. Scott was helpless to help him in this, so told him to hurry.

Blood filled his mouth as he bit into her belly. Whimpering a little, Scott calmed his wolf by telling him he was the only one that could save her. The second bite was to her leg, and that was when he noticed that Trent had shifted as well and was biting Chloe in all the same area's he was. They were working together to save her.

I'm stronger. If we don't hurry this along, we'll lose her. Thanking his brother, he told his wolf to hurry again. As they took turns biting into her flesh, he tried not to think about what they were doing, but instead thought about what was going on upstairs.

He could hear his mom and dad crying. William screaming. His grandda and grandma were there as well, and they were offering support, blankets were ready, and they had a car ready to take her home when they were finished. Then Anastasia was there, offering up her own blood.

"I'm sure that if the vamp were here, he'd do the same. But she's my friend and has been for many years. Let me help." Nodding, Scott moved back. Not too far, but enough for her to get to Chloe. "My blood is richer than yours, so it'll help save her while she converts."

As soon as Anastasia cut her wrist and put it over Chloe's mouth, he saw the fae shift. Wings appeared at her back, her face elongated and became shiny. He realized it wasn't shiny, but sparkling. The woman's entire body was covered in gems

137

and stones so small it looked like she was covered in glitter. When she looked at him, he saw the changes in her face as well.

Her eyes were dark, almost the color of old amethyst. Her lips as red as roses in his mother's garden. When she laughed, he looked at her face, her wings distracting him and his world for a few moments.

"You really didn't think I looked like a human, did you?" He shook his head. "You may speak to me now, wolf. My blood is hers now, and as you are mates, you are afforded all the things that she has."

Will she die? Anastasia said no, not any more. *I should have done this sooner, changed her. She has some of the powers that Joe gave us when she came to the family, but not all. This is not the way that I wanted her to become mate to my wolf.*

"Had you not been here, with your brother, she would surely have died. You're a good man, Scott Calhoun, and I'd be happy to call you friend as well. But you should know that you and her, you will have more than that now. Chloe has been.... I told you once that she saved me. I wasn't kidding when I told you that. Her body was broken when she gave me her blood. I think she thought that to save me would have been her last act on this earth. But to give freely as she has done numerous times, my kind has rewarded her."

How? Anastasia stood up then, her body back to the human she'd been pretending to be. *What do I owe you? I know that you said she was your friend and that you wanted to save her for that reason, but I must give you something. A boon, I think you would call it.*

"Very good, young pup. Yes. I will take one thing from you. But for now you must take your mate home and let her rest. She will be up to her old self soon, and you will need to keep her calm for a bit longer."

When she went up the stairs, he realized that Trent was still there, staring at the woman as she made her way up the stairs. He turned to him with the most comic look on his wolf's face.

Did you see that? He nodded, taking his body back so he could take Chloe home. When Trent followed him, he asked him again if he'd seen that.

"Why would I not? Sheesh, Trent, you're such a dork at times." He heard his brothers laughing and found that he loved that sound. He wanted to hear it more often, have them around him a lot more. All of his family. "Trent, I've come to a decision. I'd very much like to take you up on your offer to become your enforcer."

"Now you answer me? I asked you that four weeks ago. You told me to...I think your exact words were to go fuck myself." Scott said he'd changed his mind. "And who do I have to thank for this change of heart? The fae? Or was it your mate?"

"No. I decided all on my own. I want to spend more time with my family. I've been avoiding you guys a lot lately, and I think this is the best way to do that. Besides, my mate here is going to be the chief of police as soon as I can talk her into it, and I'll have to keep busy or go nuts."

Scott took her out to their car and laid her on the back seat. Just as he was trying to figure out how to buckle her in, Noah appeared. He offered to take her home for him and put her to bed. Scott hugged him, and as soon as Noah wrapped his arms around him, Scott felt the entire day weigh him down.

He started crying like a child, babbling about how he was a crappy mate, how he'd failed her the first time he'd had to help her. And through it all Noah held him. When he'd cried himself out, he stood up and apologized to him.

"No need for that, Scott. I've been a little down myself of late." He helped him pick up Chloe, whose heart was sounding stronger all the time. "I'll just run her home, then I'll see you there. Oh, and before I forget, you have a guest. I think him to be your new cook."

Scott was still standing there when his mom came out of the building. The fire department had been called in, she told him, and then she asked about Chloe. He told her what they'd done.

"Good for the two of you. Now, if you could manage to make me a grandmother again soon, I'll be as happy as I can be." He kissed her on the cheek and got into his car. But she wasn't done with him yet, apparently. "Scott. Are you really going to work with Trent?"

"Yes, ma'am. I think I am." She nodded and told him it was about time. Scott was still laughing about her expression when he told her he might take over the pack from him. He'd never do that, but he loved keeping her on her toes.

By the time he was pulling into his driveway, he was feeling the day again. Not as overwhelmed as he had been, but exhausted now. He thought that he could sleep for a week. He might do it while Chloe recovered. Then he was going to have to talk her into her new job.

CHAPTER 10

Chloe was sure she could do this, but she just wasn't sure she wanted to. She was still trying to figure out how she'd gotten talked into this thing, but that was going to be a conversation she was going to have later. If Scott survived his first day too. Walking back into the station she'd called home so long ago, she was sure she'd get herself killed. Again.

There were seven people, all of them wearing their street clothing and badges. She knew their names now. Not the ones on the books, but the ones they were wanted by. Each of them had a warrant out for their arrest, and she was going to bring them in. She and Anastasia were, anyway. She cleared her throat when no one moved to see what she wanted.

"If you're here to file a complaint, then you'll have to come back some other time. We aren't taking requests today." She looked over at a man she only knew as Goumas. "You go on and get yourself home now, and be careful out there. You never know what trouble might befall you."

"You should know." With a short nod to Anastasia, Chloe addressed the entire group of men there. "Bob Miles has been arrested, as have three of the men that used to work here. He will be facing a grand jury in a week. As of eight this morning, I am your new boss."

They just stared at her before bursting out laughing. The older of the men—she wasn't sure of his stage name—made his way to the counter where she was standing and leaned against it. She noted two things right away. He smelled of liquor, and he wasn't taking her seriously.

"No, you ain't. I haven't picked a new boss yet, and you surely would not be my pick." Goumas stood up and puffed out his less than impressive chest as the man in front of her continued. "You do as I said, Mrs. Calhoun, and I'll take care of things here. Just like I have been."

"You don't seem to understand. I wasn't asking for your permission to be your boss. Nor did I need your permission. I am. And I have a lot of cleaning house to do. So for now, as my first act as the new sheriff in town, you're all fired." Goumas came at her, his hand on his gun. And when he was standing no more than a foot from her, she looked him in the eyes. "You touch me, Michael Forthright, and I will tear you apart."

She knew by the look on his face when he figured out that she knew him. As he took a step back, she took one forward. If he wanted to be her first takedown, she was going to make it good.

Putting out her hand, she pressed it into his forehead. Raping his mind wasn't hard, she thought; perhaps he was just too big a shit for anyone to care what he had there. She wasn't gentle with it either. As each of his deeds came forth, she said the name of his victim as well as where it occurred. When he dropped to the floor, she staggered back a little. Luckily there was a desk right behind her.

142

"Next?" Each man there stood up. "Oh come now, you can't expect me to take you all on at once, do you? I mean, I'm just a little girly here. Isn't that what you call women you think should bow down before you and do as they're told?"

"You fucking bitch."

The man who spoke pulled out his gun, but before he could lift it she was lifting him up off the floor with just her hand. As he struggled against her hold, she addressed the room again. She'd been practicing this for two hours, and was thrilled to death she was able to do it.

"Now, as I was saying. I'm the new boss here and you are all under arrest. The Feds, as you know, have been looking for each and every one of you for years now. And lucky me, I have you all right here in my little jail." Chloe tossed the man she held away from her and watched him hit the wall behind him and slide to the floor. "Anastasia, they're all yours."

It took them nearly three hours to get the men gathered. For the most part they went along easily. There were only a couple who tried to resist. But since the men that Anastasia had brought with her were just as she was, all fae, it didn't take much to convince them that they'd live long enough to go to trial if they cooperated. It was well past midnight when every computer and other electronic piece of equipment was removed from the premises. Scott and her new family were there to help her move in.

"I don't know why we couldn't just wait and do this tomorrow." Scott told her that it looked better if she moved in right away. A show of being in charge from the very start. "I'm sure you're right, but I've had a really stressful day."

"You had a blast and we both know it." He asked her to move so that he could put in her new desk. "By the way, this is from my mom and dad. Dad has a friend who makes furniture, and he had some special compartments put in it for you."

As he showed her the two drawers that had a false bottom, she tried to think what on earth she'd use them for. Yes, they were really cool, but her mind was too tired to think. Sitting in her new chair, she told him she was done.

"Noah wants to talk to us." She shook her head. "He said that it's important. I think I've put him off long enough. He swears that it will only take a moment of our time."

"I'm not sure what he could want me for. I think he knows that I'm afraid of him still." Scott nodded and sat on the edge of her desk. "He is going to want to take some of my blood, isn't he?"

"I would say that's part of it, but not all. It comes in handy having a vamp that can find you." She said that was the problem. "What happened? I mean, you don't seem to have a problem with any other paranormal. And I know for a fact that you know a lot of them. Why vampires?"

"I'd been on the force here for about three months. I was a rookie, so I knew that whatever I ran into, I was going to get the shit end of the day's calls. This was before the entire department was taken over by thugs. Anyway, I was out on a domestic and I entered the home after two failed attempts to get someone to let me in. And there he was." Chloe shivered when she thought of that image. "The man was dead. I have no idea how I knew that, but he was. And his wife was being held by this big monstrous being. He was drinking from her. Draining her really. So I ordered him to drop the woman, and he just looked at me while he continued to kill the woman."

"He must have been invited in." She nodded. "What did you do? I'm assuming that he attacked you."

"No. He didn't attack. The woman was still alive and he

was going to take every last drop of her." She looked up at Anastasia when she entered the room with her. "Her mate had invited the vamp in; he wanted his wife dead, you see. Because she had money and he didn't."

Anastasia sat down, and Scott knew in that moment that the woman had been her. This had been the first time, he'd bet, that the two of them hooked up. She picked up the story when Chloe told her to go ahead.

"I was lonely. I took him as my husband because I was just lonely. From time to time my kind does that, takes a human to be with them until they die. It's most sad, I think, but it does take some of the loneliness away for a time." Scott asked Anastasia how long she'd been around. "Longer than generations of your family. I was around well before your sister, Joe, and her vampire, Noah. I am ancient."

He tried to wrap his mind around that. Being around for generations of families coming and going. Scott knew that Noah was very old — how old exactly he had no idea — but to think that this woman had been around longer made his head spin a little.

"And the vampire? What happened to him?" Chloe looked at her friend and waited. The story from here was for Anastasia to tell, he figured, and he looked at her while holding onto Chloe's hand. "You killed him, I'm assuming."

"I didn't." Anastasia laughed a little and nodded toward his mate. "Chloe came into the room with her gun still in her holster and ordered him to free me. He only laughed, his mouth still at my throat. But when he let me go suddenly, just dropped me to my knees, I looked at her as she stood there. She was covered from head to toe in blood. The blood that the vampire had just taken into his body from mine. My hero saved my life by killing a very old and very mean vampire.

She's stabbed him through the chest, you see."

"I don't understand." Anastasia asked him what he didn't understand. "She stabbed him through the chest with what? You said the gun never left her holster."

"I killed him with my baton; I think it's also referred to as a billy club. A baton that my father had had made for me when I graduated from the academy. He told me when he gave it to me that there were all sorts of people out there, and even more creatures that would be willing to kill me in a not so conventional way. He gave it to me to protect myself. It's made of the purest silver, and the tip of it is polished olive branch." She knew that if Scott had a vampire friend, he would understand the significance of the olive tree. "I slammed it into his chest, and as he was full of blood, it splattered over me."

"You saved Anastasia." She nodded and told him they'd been friends since. "And this vampire, you killed him and that's the reason that you're afraid of them?"

"No. I was hunted by them. For a time. I don't know why they stopped, but for a while I had to be extremely careful of everywhere I went. And they were not nice about how they treated me when they did find me." Scott stood up and started to pace her large office. "I realize that all vampires aren't alike. Hell, I've known a few that were as afraid of me as I was them. But your vampire is old and very powerful. That scares me."

"He'd never harm you." She didn't say anything and Scott turned to look at her. "He wouldn't. Not only is he my friend and respects my family, he's just not like that."

"I'm sorry." He nodded and she knew that he was talking to Noah. While she was glad that he had such a good friend, she still was afraid. So when he showed up, standing in her doorway, she wasn't surprised by that either. She simply pulled out her gun and baton and laid them on the desk. Noah just looked at the items before picking up the baton and running his fingers over not just the silver tip, but the branch that held it as well.

"His name was Patrick O'Reilly. A vampire of some age… not much, but enough that he had a few powers. He could make a weaker human do as he wanted. In the case of your friend, he was able to get into her home because the man was weak." Noah looked over at Anastasia as he continued. "You knew this as well, I think."

"Yes. We had fun. It was a nice, calm marriage. He didn't know what I was, which was why I was surprised to find out that he wished me dead. My husband had all that he wanted, and I would have given him more should he have asked." Noah nodded and looked at her as Anastasia explained. "I only heard that Patrick wanted the money that I had from one of his friends when he came for Chloe."

"Yes, I would imagine that Patrick wouldn't have let things go. Not that he would have warned his cohorts, but he would have bragged about his idea that he was going to be rich, and others would have known how he was killed. A most nasty man, that Patrick." Noah smiled then, not even bothering to hide his fangs. "The others stopped because of me. Not that I knew who you were or would become, but as soon as I took over the council, a job that I take very seriously, I ended them."

"Ended them." He only nodded. "Thank you. This doesn't mean that I'm going to be all warm and fuzzy with you, but I do appreciate you helping out a poor human."

"Human?" He looked over at Anastasia. "You have not told her what you've done for her? What both of you have done for her?"

"In the event that you didn't know this about her, she's not very receptive of people helping her. She'll be all kind and shit when you do it, but she'll berate herself over owing someone for years afterwards. I just thought I'd let her figure it out on her own."

Chloe looked at the two of them as they bantered back and forth. "Hello? Sitting right here. What did you do?" When she didn't answer her, Chloe looked at Noah. "What did she do to me?"

"You have shared it, by the way. With not just your mate, but with Trent and Joe. Joe had a great deal of magic before you came—" Chloe stood up and grabbed her baton. "While the silver will slow me, it won't kill me. And I have been around long enough to figure out precaution to that particular wood. But in answer to your question, she has given you a part of herself."

~~~

Scott realized that he wasn't alone in his new office. Hadn't been probably for a while by the looks of what the person across from him was doing. His dad was about halfway through one of the many books Scott had been given.

He'd been set up in this building yesterday, and had been told he could make it like he wanted. Today he'd come by to see what he could do to make it look less like a box than it did. Being the enforcer to a wolf as strong as Trent had perks, but being his brother too held a special kind of fun to it all. Dad laughed when he closed the book of rules he'd been reading over. Scott told him what he'd found in his book that bothered him.

"Did you know that in order for me to be his enforcer, I have to kill someone? I don't think that's going to be a negotiable thing, either." His dad said he'd done that already.

"No, I've been holed up in this office for the past two days just reading this. I'm pretty sure I would have remembered killing someone. Besides, I signed the paperwork and was handed this book of rules, so there wouldn't have been time for me to have committed mayhem and murder."

"Sure you did. And you should know that it's one of those retro laws. Anyway, you already killed for your brother... well, his mate too. To save Joe. In the bank." Scott said that he'd only been trying to save the people there. Joe was Trent's mate. "Yes, she is. But you saved them by watching his back, killing whatever came at him, and that is how you've come to have that taken care of. Ask the men in charge, they'll tell you the same thing."

Scott said nothing as he thought of Trent killing the previous alpha and how he'd been the one that kept the others, his pack really, away while he'd done it. Scott was thrilled to death to have one less thing to worry about.

"Okay. That makes sense, sort of. Thanks, Dad. You took a lot off my mind." He looked around the room that was as stark as his garage was at the moment. And realized that while his dad had been here for a while, he had no idea why. "Why are you here? I'm assuming that either you were sent, which I doubt because you never do what someone wants you to do if you can get out of it, or you have something on your mind. Which is it, old man?"

"You have no respect for me, do you, you little shit?" Scott laughed when he did. "As a matter of fact, I was sent here. By your pretty little mate. She is having some issues that.... Well, I helped her as best I could, but I don't think I did it to her satisfaction. She's a mite intense, ain't she?"

"She is. What is it you tried to help her with?" His dad moved around the room then, going to the window that

149

looked out over the streets and right into the police station. "Dad?"

"Did you know that at one time I thought myself a failure? Not with my job—no, not that—but with being a father." Scott told him he was a great father. "Because of your mom. I was never any good at being the heavy. Worse at trying to corral you boys into being good men."

"We're what we are because of the two of you. If you weren't the heavy, which I remember a few times you were, then Mom stepped in. The two of you made us just what we are today. Good men who love and respect their parents. But you didn't answer me. What did you do with my mate?"

His dad just stood there, staring out the window as if it was going to give him the answers he was searching for. And Scott knew that's what he was doing, trying to soften whatever blow he had to give him.

"Anastasia is going to be staying here." Scott told him he was trying to help her find a house to live in. "I've never known a fae, have you?"

"No. I don't think so. But according to Anastasia, there are more of them out and about than we can imagine." Scott stood up and moved to the window as well. "What's going on, Dad?"

"I don't want to live forever." Scott wasn't shocked by the statement. Scott knew that he'd been a little upset about it when he'd been told. "That mate of yours, she's been helping me adjust to this living forever. I don't know that someone would call her kind of getting me to understand helpful, but that's what she calls it. And in return, I've been helping her with becoming a better wolf. She wants to surprise you with her ability."

"I don't understand." His dad nodded but didn't clarify

for him. "How is she helping you adjust, and how are you teaching her to be a better wolf?"

"I'm going to be a grandda. I know that, but I sort of forgot about some of the things that might be a benefit to living a long time. She pointed out to me, none too gently either, that I get to see my family grow and grow from now until eternity. She also…well, I gotta tell you son, she sure can make her point in the most unhospitable way, that girl of yours." His dad rubbed his cheek while grinning. "She told me that I should be thrilled to death that I was going to be around teaching my grandkids the meaning of life. Chloe said that I could get into trouble with them; not that she thought I wouldn't, but she was pointing things out to me."

"She hit you?" His dad grinned broader and laughed a little as he nodded. "I see. She's not going to let you sit around in your own self-pity either; you know that, right?"

"Yeah, she pretty much told me to get out of the house and get busy living." He asked his dad why he thought himself a failure. "About that. I don't want to mess up my grandkids. I want them to look up to me and say, 'There goes the best grandda in the world.' I'm a feared that they're going to say, 'There goes my grandda, he sure is a weird guy.'"

"First of all, I don't think it's possible at all for you to be messing up anyone's life. I love the fact that you have a sense of humor about the oddest things. You are the only man I know that can light up a room with just a little gig. You say the oddest things at times, yes, but you make me laugh." His dad pointed out how he'd messed up recently. "Everyone does. And I don't think Mom cared as much as you did that you ran over her roses when you lost control of the mower. And I'm pretty sure, if I know you as well as I think I do, that you've made up for it."

"I bought her a garden of them." His dad nodded again. "Your mom is the best thing that ever happened to me. You know that now that you have your own mate, what it feels like to have someone to love you." Scott reached out and pulled his dad to him for a much needed hug. "I tell you, son, there ain't no better thing in the world than having kids that ain't afraid to hug you on occasion."

"Dad, I love you with all my heart." They held each other for several more minutes, neither of them saying anything. And when his dad pulled back first, Scott let him. "Now, why are you here?"

"I need me something to do. I ain't allowed to mow anymore. I should have known better than to get on that contraption in the first place. So I need me a job." Scott asked him what he wanted to do. "Well, I've been thinking on that. You know how your brother and Noelle have been hitting the antique market? Well, I was thinking of becoming an auctioneer. You know I can talk a lot more than most. Why not make some money at it?"

"An auctioneer. Okay, you're right about talking someone to death." His dad pointed out he'd only said he could talk a lot. "Yeah, Dad, you talk a man to death. It's always interesting, and you know more facts about nothing than anyone I've ever known. But what do you know about becoming an auctioneer?"

"Not a darn thing." They both laughed. "I've had my Joe looking into things for me. I don't think it will be a hardship on me. You know, the gift of gab and all. And I think your mom might be happier with me out from under her feet all the time. And my dad, he said he'd get into it with me. We might be the best of the best once we get it going."

Scott tried to imagine his dad and grandda in an auction

152

setting. There would be nothing sold; they'd be so happy to have a captive crowd that they'd be mingling more than they'd be selling. He thought about suggesting that they take in another partner, one that would actually *be* an auctioneer, and thought that would take the fun out of it for them. His grandda could out talk and out fact as well as his dad.

"I think it would be perfect for you." His dad smiled, the first real smile he'd given him since he'd gotten there. "Not only that, but I'm pretty sure that once you get it established, Noelle and Sterl can keep you supplied with business too. They run across a lot of people just wanting to get rid of lots of things."

"That's what I was thinking. You know that there are barns of crap just waiting for someone to root through. Even Joe, she told me that Noah has a warehouse full of things from so long ago that they don't even remember it." He was glad to see his dad excited. Then he frowned. "Chloe. I forgot to tell you. Darn it all to Hades and back. She said for you to bring home some steaks, and she was gonna have to tell you something. It's about my lessons, I'm sure. So don't you be raining on her garden just because I slipped up and told you about her."

Looking at the time on his phone, he realized it was getting late. Giving his dad another hug, he made his way to the store as he thought about his dad being an auctioneer. The man was a wonder, he'd give him that. But he just didn't see this thing working out the way he thought. It would be more of a social event than his mom's tea parties in the spring. Scott was still laughing as he picked up a bouquet of flowers for his pretty little mate.

CHAPTER 11

"So you know how to cook and bake." The man grinned at her, then told her he had a great deal of experience. Chloe looked over at Anastasia when she laughed. "I know nothing about hiring someone. Perhaps you can tell me just why it is that I need to hire this man."

"Okay. Benton, I want you to show our young friend here why." The man nodded, and in an instant had a plate of cookies in one hand and a glass of tea in the other. "He's magical. You should have known that I'd never leave you alone to fend for yourself."

"So he doesn't really cook, but makes things." Benton told her that he could cook, he had just wanted to show off. "Okay, when you show off again, maybe instead of cookies you could make some scones? Noelle makes them sometimes, and I've fallen in love with the lemony ones."

The plate of cookies was replaced with scones. Warm ones that looked like they'd just been baked, the steam rolling off the top of them picture perfect. And they had a lemony smell to them that made her mouth water. The glass of tea was now a cup of hot, the cup so beautiful and delicate that she didn't want to pick it up.

"My lady, I would also like to take over the construction of the household." Since she had no idea what that meant, so long as it didn't make her have to use a hammer again, she told him fine. "Shall I take care of ordering foodstuff as well? You have a few staples, but not enough to sustain a household this big."

"There are only the two of us. Not including you. How much in the way of staples do you think we'll need?" His only reply was plenty. When he left them to their tea and scones, Chloe looked over at her friend. "You changed me. I'm not the same as the rest of them."

"No, you're not. Neither is your mate." Chloe looked down at the crumbs on her plate, not even sure if she'd eaten one or two of the pastries. The plate they were on seemed to replace each one they ate. "I have some things I should like to tell you. Are you ready for them?"

"No. I've decided just this minute that I would prefer to live the rest of my life in the dark about a great many things." Anastasia laughed. "I'm being serious here. You have no idea how freaked out I am about some of this stuff."

"I'm sure you'll get used to it. I know that it's a lot, but I need you and Scott for something." She asked her if it was dangerous. "No. Not at all. More of a perk job."

"Perk? I don't know why, but I don't think I'm going to think of this job as a perk." She laughed again, and this time Chloe joined her. "You know that I'd do anything in the world for you. You saved my life as many times as you think I saved yours. I owe you."

"You owe me nothing but friendship. And that is what this request is that I ask of you, a friendship sort of deal."

Chloe waited for her to tell her, but she changed the subject. "Did you know that there are several hundred acres around this land that are sitting idle?"

"Yes. I mean, I really didn't know there was that much, but I knew there was a lot of land. The area has been in a funk, I guess. There are new businesses coming in. One in particular is nearly done with his building." Anastasia only nodded. "You're making me crazy. What is it?"

"Doug Coulier, he's the owner of the company." Chloe said she thought so. "I should like to meet him. With you there. I have a plan for his business, and I would enjoy having you as well as young Noelle there."

"Are you going to kill him?" Chloe had been kidding, but when Anastasia said nothing back, she got concerned. "Please tell me that I'm not going to be the witness to a murder. Or I swear to Christ, you're on your own from now on."

"Nothing like that, not if he will listen. I need to convince him to hire a few of my people." Chloe asked her why. "Because what he is doing to the earth and the air around the building that his company will be using is very harmful to my kind. I should like for him to hire a few of my people so that they might keep him from harming us anymore."

"I see. And your people there, what will that do to help your kind? Or do you want me to know?" Anastasia shook her head. "Okay, I can live with that. But why do you need us to be there with you? I'm assuming that you think we can convince him to help you?"

"Nay, I think him a man who knows what he is about. This project, like so many that might come here, will boost the economy, but it will also harm others such as myself. I know that he is taking many precautions for pollution and such, but there is so much more that he could be doing." Chloe asked her when she wanted to go. "Now. The timing is right for us."

Before she could ask her what she meant, Noelle knocked on the back door. And soon after that, a gentleman, a well-dressed man wearing a very expensive suit, came as well. He said his name was Nash and nothing more. When Anastasia said nothing about him, Chloe didn't ask. There were some things, she'd come to realize, that she really didn't want to know.

Doug was willing to meet with them when they arrived. He was polite, but Chloe knew that something was wrong. And when he closed his phone after a very terse call, she asked him again.

"I'm not having a good day." Chloe said she could see that. "There is an EPA guy here that has been hanging around for a week now. It's almost as if he's looking for trouble so that he can pounce on it. I'm so sorry about this."

Chloe thought the meeting was over, but no one moved to stand. Anastasia cleared her throat after several seconds and asked if she might help. If there was an answer to her query, Chloe missed it because she just disappeared. Doug looked at her when Anastasia was gone.

"I don't understand." She laughed and said she didn't either. "I've been extremely pressed to get this building done, but we're running into more trouble than I thought. Nothing to do with the land or the building, but it's almost as if every government agency wants to come in and put me further and further behind. You have no idea the list of shit this guy this morning gave me."

"I should like to stay here and help you." Chloe glanced at Nash as he continued talking to Doug. "I will help you in ways that you cannot even fathom. But I should like a favor in return."

"Is this why these men are here?" It took her a moment to understand that he thought that Nash was responsible for his troubles. "Because if it is, then I'll just close up this place and walk away if you think to blackmail me."

Nash looked at her for an explanation. "Essentially, it's coercion. It involves a threat about one thing or another, and if they don't meet their demands, then they'll cause harm or something like that. There was this case where a little boy had been kidnapped. And when the parents did what he wanted, he was to give the boy back. They wanted this man to stop producing alcoholic beverages because their son had been killed by drinking and driving. They were blaming the manufacturer, not their son."

"I've no wish for a child to be harmed." Nash looked at Doug. "I only wish for you to allow me to stay here so that I might help you. I don't have any need of your money or children, but only wish to make it so that nothing in our area is hurt."

"You just want to come here and help me for no charge." Nash nodded. "And what will you require when I have the building up and running. To take it from me?" Doug seemed to realize that he was being rude and shook his head. "I'm sorry. I don't know why I'm being this way other than I've not been sleeping well, nor have I had a decent meal in days. The house that I'm renting is a nice place, but it's hard to get home to relax and eat when this is going on."

Anastasia returned then and told him he'd have no more trouble with the EPA. She also told him that she'd taken care of the two other firms that had been in the building. Then she asked about Nash.

"He said he can help me. But he doesn't want money or anything else." Doug stretched his neck. "I'm beginning to think that this was a major mistake."

"You'll need to plant flowers around the acreage beyond your parking lot. Trees too would be nice. And while the roof is being finished, solar panels will go a long way to making your costs lower, as well as helping the lands around you." Doug asked Anastasia why that was important. "Because I am fae, and you are harming the green around you. The trees are suffering, as are the flowers and grasses. Without them, we cannot survive. We will have to go to war with you should you not help us."

"Fae?" Doug looked at Noelle. "I had no idea there were such a thing as fae. I mean, I've heard of them but.... Why am I just now hearing about this?"

"I had no idea until today." Noelle stood up and started to pace the room as she continued. "How much will he save in the first year if he puts in panels like you said? I mean, a ball park figure."

The total was much higher than she'd thought it would be. Then Nash listed not just the cost of putting them in, but also the savings that he would get in putting them in now rather than later.

"Water can be heated this way as well. Enough so that your emissions from the gas used to heat it would go down significantly. Then there is the shade from the trees, the fauna from the landscaping...all this will improve workers' mental abilities, as well as give the faeries and brownies something to feast upon." Doug asked him about the smaller creatures. "The faeries will protect you in ways that you should never have to worry about your staff. The brownies, while a small group of beings, can clean your building from top to bottom in less time than it would take an entire staff to do so. And a much better job."

160

"How much will that cost?" Nash told him that the flowers and the land surrounding the building would be payment enough for them. "So I plant a few flowers and they'll come and clean for me? I don't think that's terribly much, do you?"

"For them you are giving them hope of having a land plentiful of foods. The trees will provide places for them to raise their families without the fear of being killed by large machinery coming in." Nash took out a thick file and handed it to Doug. "These ladies have been kind enough to help us enter your fine establishment by setting up this meeting. And to see what you have done here. You are working to becoming a green warehouse, and you have done an excellent job thus far, but I can take you further. If you would allow me to do so."

As they worked out the details, Noelle taking notes, Nash telling Doug that the people he had in place would help as well, Chloe looked over at Anastasia. She looked sad and she asked her quietly about it.

"This will help so many, you know that, don't you? I mean, not just the man here, but all the creatures that have about given up hope of having any sort of place to call their own." Chloe asked her what else was bothering her. "The man there, he is my mate."

~~~

Scott had never enjoyed running in the woods with his brother as much as he was today. Chloe had an appointment in town with the Feds about her new job, and he'd been bored out of his mind at home waiting for her to return. Then Trent and Randal had shown up and asked if he'd run with them.

Tomorrow was going to be hard on Chloe, he knew it. The building that Scott had purchased from his grandda earlier had been closed off tighter than he'd seen a building. Not only were there chains on the doors, but two armed guards patrolled the place at all times.

William was mourning the death of his son. Not in the way Scott thought that a man would, but that he no longer had anyone to come and bail him out. Not that there was any money for bail, but William was pissed that there wasn't anyone gathering something up for him. According to him, the Calhoun family had ruined him. Scott saw Randal and was ready to pounce on him when he felt the earth beneath his nails shift.

Not yet. Scott felt his wolf freeze at the voice in their head. *Not just yet, my lord. He will change direction in a moment.*

Sure enough, Randal moved to his right and had Scott leapt at him, he would have fallen head over ass, making a fool of himself. When Scott's wolf lay in the dry leaves, Scott asked who the person was.

Person? I'm not a person, my lord, but the earth beneath your feet. Should you dig your nails a little deeper for us, we will have a better connection. His wolf just yawned and didn't move. *I see you are going to be stubborn, my young pup. I promise you, should you do as I ask, I will reward you greatly with the knowledge on how to take down the big alpha.*

Taking his time, his wolf did stretch out his paws and dig his thick nails into the soil beneath him. Scott felt the connection immediately. He was pretty sure that the wolf in him did as well.

I'm not sure that taking down the big alpha is a plan I can live with at the moment. Not without knowing who you are and how you contacted me. Well, us I guess. The laughter in his head had him smiling. There was something so childlike about it that he was nearly charmed by it. *Please, I don't know you, nor what your plans are.*

162

I am of the earth, as I said. Anastasia, she has given us all the ability to speak with you, to help you in any way that we can. I was with your young mate today when she was out in the earth. She is much better now that she's listening to me. Scott wondered why Chloe hadn't told him about talking to the earth. *She did not know, my lord. I believe she thinks us a figment of her mind. Or perhaps a part of it. I did not want to frighten her, so I let her believe what she needed. But you are stronger in that you are aware of other creatures that can be out there. The young mistress, she is as new to this as the grass that grows in the spring.*

But she's aware of fae. She's a good friend of Anastasia. The earth said that was correct. *Then how is she not receptive to your talking to her?*

She is still young in her knowledge of us. It has only been a few winters since she met the queen. And Anastasia, she has given you both a great deal of herself, but you have grown up knowing what you are, who you will become. She is yet but a babe. Scott said he could see that. Then what she'd said occurred to him. But before he could ask, the earth spoke again. *Your alpha, he is like you? A brother?*

Yes. He is my oldest brother. Randal is here as well. He was the first person you warned me about. The earth said nothing, so he asked her about the queen. *Who is the queen you were talking about? Is it Anastasia? Is she the queen of fae?*

Her sister. Anastasia was the sister to the queen of fae? Christ, that would make her a princess. *You should stop thinking so hard, my lord. I think you are disturbing the land around you. Breathe slowly and I will tell you when to pounce.*

When she told him now, Scott and his wolf leaped up and grabbed Trent by the neck. It was play so he didn't hurt him, but he did take him down twice before he was able to get free. As their wolves stood there staring at each other, they were both surprised when their dad came out of the dark woods laughing.

"He got you good, didn't he? Darn near wet my socks when I saw him get you. Jumped out like he knew you were there." The voice in his head cautioned him from sharing just yet that he did have help. "I tell you, I never would have believed it had I not seen it with my own eyes."

"Dad, he was lucky, that's all." Trent wasn't pissed but he was shocked. So was Scott, but he took his body back when his brothers did. "I guess I owe you dinner. Last man standing gets to pick, too."

"How about we all come over to the house and we'll have a cook out?" Scott explained how Chloe was stressing about the foundation being opened in the morning. "That way we can have some fun, make her laugh, and she'll feel better."

"Excellent idea. I'll call your grandparents and your momma right now. That'll be good. I hear you have yourself a fine cook." He told his dad that all he'd had to eat at the house so far was cereal. "Cereal? You mean that processed crap that they put in boxes that ain't worth the dirt of a land fill? That crap?"

"Yes, Dad, that crap. I have crap like that every morning. My particular favorite is the crap that has little yogurt balls in it. Tasty." His dad glared at him. "It's not crap. And Chloe likes it. So I eat it so I can have breakfast with her every morning."

"Oh well. Not the best stuff, but that's sure a good reason." His dad's approval made him smile. "Mom said that she's picking up a few things. I'd say it's gonna be a lot, so just be ready. And when we get there, I'm going to have to have a little talk with that girl of yours."

They made their way to the house, and almost as soon as they let Benton know that others were coming for dinner, he said he had it taken care of. Scott wasn't worried in the least bit that there wouldn't be enough food, or that it would be anything but delicious. He knew that the man was fae; Anastasia had sat him and Chloe down and explained to them what he was, why he was there, and even the extent of his magic. Which was a great deal of it. But she'd never mentioned being the sister of the queen.

"Benton was at one time a part of a great army of his kind. He and his men fought wars so great that many lives were lost, and the land suffered greatly for it. When he retired, his mind and body no longer able to deal with such horrors, he took to cooking. For a time, and he probably won't tell you this, he was considered one of the greatest cooks of all time." Chloe asked her why their home, why now. "Because I love you both so much."

It was a fantastic answer, but not the real one he'd bet. Anastasia did indeed love them, he had no doubt about that, but he was sure that the reasons she gave for Benton being in their home wasn't the honest answer.

Dinner was a great success. The steaks were perfectly cooked for each of them, and baked potatoes were served with not just sour cream, but thick chucks of bacon fried crisp, green onions, and cheese. Green beans with ham, corn on the cob, and the freshest tea. Biscuits too. Not as good as Joe made, but they were right up there, and Scott noticed that Trent was hoarding a few under his plate. The man had a very strange obsession with biscuits. Just when they were all groaning about how stuffed they were, Benton brought out pies.

Banana cream was Scott's favorite. Ginger snap crust with vanilla pudding was the only way to make it as far as he was concerned. But there were cherry and apple, as well as Boston cream, just like his grandma used to make for them on the holidays.

"I'm telling you right now, Benton. If you ever want to leave this son of mine, you got yourself a place in my house. You and Meggie, you can take turns making this old man fatter." Mom smacked him on the arm. "Oh Chrissie love, you cannot tell me that's not about the best throw together meal you ever ate."

"It was, but you cannot be taking away their cook right under their noses. You should do it later, when no one is around." When she leaned over to Dad and whispered loudly in his ear, they all laughed. "Double his pay, and give him perks if you have to."

Scott thought it was the best time they'd all had in a while. Even his lovely mate looked a little more relaxed. Tomorrow was going to be a long hard day.

CHAPTER 12

William wasn't sure where they were headed. All he'd been told was that he should dress in the clean orange jumper they gave him or he'd go naked. It wasn't a way to treat someone like him, and he was going to have to make calls. William had hoped that one of the many attorneys that he'd met over the years would have come to see him about this injustice, but not a single one of them had.

Yesterday they'd laid his son to rest. The stupid little fucker had killed himself. If he was going to do something so stupid that was fine, but he should have at least waited until his father was taken care of. George had never been that good of a boy, but he'd been useful. Most of the time he'd used him as a scapegoat, and lately it had gotten so easy to convince his son what a terrible person he was because of the drugs.

Keeping his son suppled with enough drugs to keep him out of his hair had been expensive. With all the money problems they'd had of late, that wasn't working out so well either. But like all good Flynn men, when George had wanted something, he would figure out a way to get it.

When they pulled up in front of his house, William thought for sure that someone had finally come to their senses. To lock a poor man up after his son had killed himself was a crime. He'd thought that one up while he'd been eating his paltry dinner last night. As he was being let out of the car, he looked around and took his first deep breath since he'd been arrested.

"Mr. William George Flynn?" William looked over at the man standing next to him. "You are William Flynn, are you not?"

"I am. Who are you and what is it you want? I've only just been released and I don't have time for any sales pitches. I want to.... My son has recently passed away, and I want to grieve in private." He put out his hands when the officer that had driven him home came toward him. "If you'll remove these now, I'll just go inside."

"Remove them? I don't think so. We're here to get some information from you. Then you're going right back to jail to await your trial." He asked him what he was being accused of. "Well, for starters, murder. Then there is insurance fraud. You also—"

"Wait a minute. Just wait. I didn't kill anyone. And what insurance? I never made a claim." Not for lack of trying, he thought. "Explain to me just what is going on here."

His wife had had a nice insurance policy, but since he couldn't prove that she was dead without getting himself in deep shit, he'd had to let it lay on his dresser and wait the seven years to have her declared dead.

"We found her body." William looked at the man who had approached him first, certain that he'd heard him wrong. "Just this morning we dug up the lower levels of the Flynn computer shop, and you'd be surprised how much we found there. Not only the remains of your wife, but the lawyer that you claimed she ran off with, as well as her father. When you go on a spree, you really do it up nicely, don't you? By the way, the next time you kill someone and bury them under a building, you should be more careful of finger prints on the weapon you leave behind."

"My wife is gone." The man nodded and smiled at him. "No, I mean she ran off with our attorney. I told the police that. Several times over the years."

"Yes you did. But I'm here to tell you that you've lied all along, and that we've found her body and that of her father, James Porter, and the family attorney, David Taft." The man leaned back against the car that he'd come to his nightmare in. "Several years ago there was a hit and run out on Route Forty. Do you know anything about that?"

"Hit and run? No, why should I? I don't drive that way. When I have to go anywhere, I have a driver for that." He tried to think if there was anything in the house, anything they might have found that would lead them to where the car had been abandoned. "My son. It's too bad you can't ask him about it. George liked to drive too fast, and the roads out there by the mill are perfectly suited for that sort of thing. What with the road being as straight as an arrow and all."

The man said nothing, and William asked again who he was. "You should really shut up now. I mean, just now you've given me enough information to know that somehow you're involved in the death of Mike Davis. Even without your cooperation, I have someone here that can get the rest of what we need."

"What do you mean? I've never given you anything of the sort. I want you to release me." The man told him that wasn't happening. "Then take me back to my cell. But you should know this...as soon as they release me, I'm going to go after you and take you for all that I can."

"You mean like you did with your poor wife? What is it she did to you? Expected you to be faithful to her? I think I would have too if I had been her. Was it that she cut off your spending? Sucks to have to follow a budget when you feel there is more than enough to go around, isn't it?"

Closing his mouth, biting his tongue so he'd not say a word, William began to worry. This man knew things. Not only that, but William was pretty sure that not only did he know where the car was that he'd used to kill the officer, but that he also had gotten it. William looked around…he needed help. And he'd take it any way that he could get it. Seeing the Calhoun men standing in a circle, he stomped his way to them. He got no more than a few feet when he was stopped by the police.

"This is all your doing, isn't it?" The elder Calhoun just stared at him. "You think you can get by with planting bodies in my building and making me look bad? Well, you can't. And as soon as I get out of this mess, I'm going to own you."

"You can't even afford a good attorney, you moron. How do you expect to take me on and win?" William saw red, literally. His vison was blurred with his anger, and he was sure that he was having a stroke. "You'd best take care of yourself there, Flynn. Once you get in the big house, you're going to be someone's girlfriend right away."

"I've done nothing wrong. It was all George. The moron was so stoned all the time he could barely hold down a job." Things started racing in his mind, and he was having a hard time making one of them stick long enough for him to think. "Look. Now that George is no longer with us, why don't you stop this nonsense? We'll just forget the whole thing and let it go back to the way it was before. You'll let me rent the bookstore and I'll be able to make a living. Now that my son is gone, I have a need for the quiet life."

"It was a computer store, not a bookstore. And I'm pretty sure that you'll be living the quiet life from now on. A nice little cell with no body but big Ben there to keep you company." William asked him who Ben was. "I don't know. I was making up a name of the roomie you're going to have while in prison. Christ, the apple sure didn't fall far from the tree with your family, did it?"

"Got it." They all turned toward the man who had shouted. "Black Porsche belonging to William Flynn. I have the VIN numbers as well as the keys. I've already sent a man over to see if it's still there."

His car. The one that he'd been driving the night he'd just killed his wife. William dropped to his knees when the pain in his head took his breath away. The pounding of his heart was reverberating in his head, and he could hear his blood rushing through his veins. Then when a finger touched his forehead, it was as if a plug had been pulled, and his entire well being felt renewed. He looked up at the person who had given him such relief and fell back on his ass. Christ, it was a giant fucking bug.

"Not a bug, William Flynn, but a fae. I came to heal you so that you'd stand trial." She leaned down to his level, her purple eyes level with his. When she did that, he thought she looked familiar but wasn't sure. "It's me, your friendly pain in the ass FBI agent. I'm happy that a lot of people will get closure with you getting your ten minutes of fame, and I for one will be glad for your demise. Because as surely as we are here, you will die a very painful death when you go to prison."

"No, I can't go to prison. I have things I need to get done." She only grinned at him and he felt his anger surge. "I don't know what sort of trickery you're playing here, but I won't be pulled into your fun. You tell them you've made a mistake. My wife ran off with someone. My son, he's the one that killed that officer. I hid it, yes, but he was my only child. I had to keep him safe."

"Is that why you made a deal with his drug dealer? One that would supply your son with a near endless supply of cocaine? Or was it the deal that you made with the man who drove the murder weapon to Virginia and put it in that barn? Bad news there, I'm afraid. He left a nice note in the car for whoever found it with the money that you paid him. He told how you'd made him drive the car away, and it wasn't until he was nearly to the drop off point that he realized that you'd killed a cop. He was a bad man, but he didn't want to go down for the murder of an officer of the law. Besides, he didn't think he'd live long enough to spend the payoff anyway, not with the way you were committing murder like it was your job." William was so fucked if he didn't think of a way to get out of this mess. "I'll be seeing you when you're jailed, William Flynn. You and I are going to have some fun for what you put my friend through."

"I want to make a deal. I want to talk to you about a deal." When she started laughing, a not so friendly sort of manic laughter, he stood up. "I want to confess for a deal."

The bug simply disappeared. He stood there, his body shaking for all the things they could charge him for, and knew that if he was smart, he'd let the state kill him. It might be a great deal easier than having the bug taking care of him.

~~~

Scott felt the sweat bead on his back. He was glad now that he'd taken his shirt off when he'd entered their play room. Not that the air conditioning at full blast was making him any

172

less hot and bothered, however. He looked at the woman in front of him. Christ, he could easily drop to his knees and beg her to stand like this forever.

When they'd first entered their playroom, she'd become the slave that he wanted. Head down, arms loose at her sides. For all intents and purposes, she looked docile, her body soft and ready for him. But he could smell her need and see how much it was costing her to be in such a cooled room.

Her body was clothed in a simple white robe that was as sexy as it was revealing. Nothing under it as far as he could see. No panties marred her perfect ass, and her nipples were standing erect against the sheer material that lay over them. He had to let out a long breath before he could speak.

"What is your duty?" She said nothing. He'd not given her permission to speak to him. Scott was wishing now that he'd not suggested that she read up on their kind of play. "Speak."

"To serve you in any way that you wish, Master." His cock stretched and he became more painfully aware of his own needs. He was going to do this, make her his slave even if it killed him. Which he was pretty sure it was going to. Especially after telling her to strip.

Leading her to the cross, he tied her to it. Scott made sure that he touched her as much as he could. A brush of his hand over her ass, his mouth touching her spine. He felt like he'd run a marathon by the time he had her strapped to the equipment.

Going to his cabinet to get away from her for a moment, he blindly looked inside. She was doing well, better than he could have hoped for. And here he was like a first timer, wondering what the fuck he'd gotten himself into. Reaching into the cabinet, he pulled out the first thing he touched, and nearly lost it when he saw what it was.

The whip wasn't long…about ten inches from tip to handle. Made of the softest leather, it fit perfectly in his hand. Turning to go back to her, to use whatever means possible for her to have the best sex of her life, he could only stare at her.

Her back was beautiful. The long indentation of her spine curved along her back to her ass like an artist had done it. With her shoulders back, he could see the curve of her breast, her belly pressed against the padded metal. The flare of her hips from her chest gave him the idea that he could easily span her waist with his hands, she was that tiny.

Muscles in her arms were stretched out, her fingers curled into the leather that wrapped around her slender wrists. There was a mark on her arm, just above her elbow, that he knew was a gunshot scar. They'd both been surprised when they saw it; he'd only just told her that all scars would go away after she was converted. Yet there it was, like a badge of honor.

Her legs were strong. He knew this too. When he took her against any surface he could find, she would ride him tightly, her delicate feet at his back as he slammed his cock deep inside of her. There wasn't a moment that went by that he didn't think of places to fuck her, ways to make her scream out his name.

Scott moved to her, his body hard with need. Not just to take her—he would do that—but to make her come over and over until she was exhausted. Then he'd take her again, just because he could. Running the tails of the leather down her back to the curve of her ass, he smiled when she shivered.

"Who do you belong to?" She said she was his. Slapping the leather over her ass, he leaned down and kissed the marks it had made. "I did not give you permission to speak, slave."

He smacked her again. Then twice more. As he was

moving to abuse her other cheek, he saw a trickle of cream running down her thigh. Sliding his fingers over the hot juices, he rubbed them over the marks at her ass.

He marked her back then, small streaks of his handiwork seeming to call out to him. Licking them, running his tongue over each of the marks he'd made, he cupped his cock. If he didn't get some relief soon, he was going to die, he thought. But his wolf needed his time before Scott took his. He let his wolf come forth.

His wolf moved to the front of the cross. He was as aggressive as he was; his wolf enjoyed his mate as rough as he did sometimes. So when he moved up on the platform, just so his head was at her pussy, Scott wasn't surprised when he nipped at her thigh rather than taking her.

Scott could smell her blood as it ran down her leg. He wasn't surprised that she didn't cry out; the bite, while drawing blood, hadn't been deep. As his wolf licked her pussy, he knew that Chloe was enjoying herself as much as his big wolf was.

As soon as his wolf had his fill of her, if that was even possible, Scott took his body back. He stood watching her as she breathed deeply, her heart pounding. Leaning into her throat, he licked the pulse there, almost tasting how close she was to coming for him.

Scott never said a word as he let her go. As much as he wanted to fuck her here, with her arms and legs tied wide apart, he also knew that too long stretched out like she was could harm her. And as much as he loved causing her sexual pain, he didn't want her to be physically hurt if he could help it.

Helping her to stand on her own, Scott rubbed her arms and legs when she looked to be unsteady. But her pussy called to him and he buried his mouth over her. She was so wet, so hot, that he nearly came from only his first taste.

Scott nibbled on her clit, took her nether lips into his mouth and suckled them too. Sliding his fingers up her leg and into her sheath, he was rewarded with copious amounts of her cream, spicy with her scent. He wanted her to come like this, with his mouth at her core. Scott also wanted her to win her battle, the one he knew that she was fighting to keep in check for him.

He stood then, his mouth still covered in her juices, and kissed her. He was hungry, more so because he could taste how she felt about the way he was treating her. Stepping back, he watched her bite her lip, breathing hard as he was. He was going to break her, he thought, make her not want to play again if he didn't help.

Picking her up, he loved when her body wrapped around his, her legs at his hips, arms around his shoulders. Sliding into her, he felt her tighten around him, her body stretching to accommodate his invasion. As he fucked her, bringing her body to his only to pull back, he walked to the wall on wobbly legs. Never saying a word to her, he pressed her to it and fucked her with all his strength.

She'd be sore, he knew this. He would be as well. But he needed to dominate her. Make her understand just how painful he needed it, how hard he had to take her. And when she dug her nails into his back, Scott felt blood trickle down and it made him wild with the need to come.

"Come. Now."

She exploded around him, strangling his cock as he pounded her. Leaning to her mouth, he offered her his own, and when she bit him, he tore at her shoulder just as savagely as he was taking her.

His release, such a tame mundane word for how he came, seemed to take everything from him. Darkness engulfed him for several seconds. His heart stopped beating enough that he felt dizzy, and when he came a second, then third time, Scott felt his knees weaken and his body just fall.

When he woke he was alone on the floor. He sat up carefully, knowing that he was lucky that he'd not hurt himself. Standing required him to hold onto the closest piece of equipment, and he unsteadily made his way to the bathroom just off the playroom. There he found Chloe just standing under the hot steam.

"Are you all right?" She turned and looked at him, her face red from crying. "Oh honey, I'm so sorry. I never meant to hurt you like that."

"No, you don't understand. That was...I don't think I have any words to describe how wonderful that was." She held him when he stepped into the water with her. "I'm sore, I won't lie about that, but I feel like I've been fucked by the best and came out on top."

Scott held her in his arms, rubbing what he could feel of the tight muscles of her back. "Then why are you crying, love?"

"Joe called while you were resting." He didn't want to know and he did too. "She said that the car had enough evidence on it to say that it was used to kill my dad."

He held her until she stopped crying again. Then he washed her hair and scrubbed down her body with the big sponge she'd gotten for them. As he was helping her dry off, rubbing the big fluffy towel over her, he started talking. Scott felt like he needed to say something to her to cheer her up.

"The ground spoke to me the other day. I had no idea that was even possible or that I didn't dream the whole thing up, but I was able to get the jump on Trent—not an easy feat by the way—and my dad saw it. Then I was told not to tell them how I'd done it. I'm not sure why, but I guess she didn't want them to make fun of me." Chloe asked him why he thought it was a woman. "I don't know. Because she was smart and funny. Not that men aren't, but in my experience, women are far superior to men in thinking and having a good sense of humor."

"I think she might have spoken to me as well." Scott told her that she had, but didn't want her to freak out. "I do not freak out. But she was guiding me, I think. Your dad was there with me. Not as a wolf, but he stood by my side while I got the hang of just being a wolf. I had no idea it was going to be so hard trying to go from a human to a four-legged person."

"Most people forget that it's different to walk on four after being on two for so long. I think, because we were born as wolves, that it sort of came natural to us." After she wrapped the towel around her body, he did the same to his own, wrapping it around his hips. Then he picked up the hair brush that had also been added to this room. "I want to go shopping today. I mean, for things we need to make this our home. Benton has done a great job getting the house in order, but we don't have anything personal here. Things that we've picked out."

"All right. But if you don't mind, I'd like to go by my dad's house. There are a few things there that I'd like to bring here. I think…it's time I did something with it too." He asked her what she wanted to do. "I don't know. I was thinking that someone needs to fill it. With a family, love, and understanding. Not that we didn't, Dad and I, but it's a house of memories for me now. Good ones, don't get me wrong, but sad all the same."

"I understand. And yes, whatever you want to bring here, it'll be perfect. I bought some things, just a few actually, because I was going to do the work first. But lucky for us, we have Benton." She looked up at him and smiled a watery type of a smile. "I love you, Chloe. I'm so sorry about your dad. Hopefully we can get some justice on this."

"I think it sort of reopens the wounds of him being gone. I wasn't over it, but the pain was a great deal lessened by the years. This just makes it all seem like it happened yesterday again." He told her he understood. "All right, let's get this going and see to the house. Do you suppose one of your brothers might want it?"

"Randal." He had no idea where the house was, how big it was, or anything about it, but his brother had been saying that he wanted his own home, a place he could go that wasn't shared with seventy other people. "He was just telling me that he wants out of the apartment scene. I think it's the fact that he's around kids all day long, and there are a great many of them in his complex. Even though it's supposed to be for adults only."

They made their way out after having a huge lunch. Scott was happy that Benton was living with them if for no other reason than they were certainly eating better. And they were having fun eating some of the strangest things he'd ever eaten. Okay, maybe not strange for some people, but they were for him. Like roasted Brussel sprouts and grilled pizza.

He called his brother Randal and asked him when he got off work. Being a teacher was a full time job for him, as he had just started teaching basic computer skills at the local warehouse to help adults update resumes and fill out job applications.

"I'll see you there at five. Then maybe we can have some

dinner. I'd like something that's not microwaved or served in a box." Scott told him what they were having at home and invited him over. "I'd love that. Maybe I can get that guy of yours to make me up a few leftover bags. I'd eat that through the week instead of fending off single and not so single moms to help me out."

Scott was still laughing as they got into their car. Yes, he thought, his brother was already having trouble with the ladies.

CHAPTER 13

Chloe moved around the house, touching things that she'd not thought of in years. Scott and Randal were in the garage, the lure of the cars there making them a little insane to explore. The blanket that had laid over her and her dad's feet when they'd watched television together was still there. Pretty much everything had been left exactly where he had left it that fateful morning.

His ashtray was no longer filled with mints. Her dad had given up smoking when she'd been born, but hadn't gotten rid of the collection of ash trays that he had. Some were older than he had been, having been given to him by his own dad.

The television was gone, as well as his computer. Her father was the only person she knew that only had a cell phone because she'd made him. The phone that had hung in the kitchen when she'd been living there had been replaced with a cordless, but even that was out of date now. She made her way to the kitchen, just to see if things had been done the way he'd wanted.

The kitchen had been outdated, he told her when he

bought it. And as he worked a lot of hours, it had taken him a long time to get things going. Just before he'd been killed, her dad had decided to have some professionals come in and finish up. It was the last time she'd been in the house, and the last bit of work that had been done on it.

The cabinets were beautiful in this room. They weren't the open glass kind that some people preferred. Her dad had said that he didn't want anyone knowing his business. If he wanted them to see what he had there, he'd just open the doors. The stove and the fridge were state of the art ten years ago, but were now as outdated as the rest of the house. She looked over at Randal and Scott when they entered the house.

"My dad loved this house." Randal told her he was sorry for her loss and she nodded. "I'd like to gift it to you. It's going to need a lot of work and updates, but I think my dad would love for someone like you to have it."

"I can't let you do that, Chloe. I really like the house and all, but I can't let you give it to me." She asked him why not. "Because it's your house. That is more than likely what your dad would have wanted you to do."

"No. not my dad. He would have told me that I need to move on. Not just move on, but to get busy living." She grinned. "Did you know that at one time he was going to be a teacher? He was going to retire from the job and try his hand at teaching. I think he would have been great at it. But my dad had a special place in his heart for teachers. My mom was one."

Chloe could see that he was interested, but when he looked at his brother, she knew he was going to turn her down. Scott shook his head at him before backing her up.

"This house needs someone to come in and enjoy it. It's been sitting here long enough. If you don't take it, Randal, then someone else will. Someone that won't appreciate the things done to it now. Nor will they understand that the person who lived here was a great man." Randal looked at her as Scott continued. "She and I talked it over. And when she asked me which of my brothers would enjoy this house — not buy it, not want to purchase it, but enjoy it — I thought of you. You need this place for a lot of reasons, but I think the house needs you for just as many."

"Look, just look around with me. Let me tell you things about the house that no realtor will tell you about. Like the little cubby hole in the bedroom at the top of the stairs. The panic room that was here when he bought it, as well as the wine cellar that few would care about." Randal said he would look but that didn't mean he was taking it. "All right. Let's start right here in this room."

Going to the door that served as a pantry door, she opened it up and then closed it tightly. Pressing the button on the top of the door, she opened it once again, and this time the hidden safe was revealed.

"He wanted a place that would be okay to put his guns. By the time this was added I was out of the house, but he also didn't want neighbors or other children finding his gun. Dad took gun safety very seriously." She moved into the pantry, and when they were both inside, she showed them the place in the floor that opened. "Not much use for this anymore, and I'm sure it's not on any plans, but the previous owners put in a bomb shelter about ten years before they sold to my dad. I would go down there and play house when he was at work."

They didn't enter the large area, but she told him of the kitchen, living quarters, as well as the hydro gardens that still worked as far as she knew. She also told him that the place was heated by a separate heating unit from the one on the house, and the power down there was all solar. Her dad had done that part.

"He wasn't what you'd call a fixer upper sort of person, but he could read instructions and follow them to get the job done." She took him to the dining room, one of her dad's favorite rooms. "The cabinets were brought from a couple of old farm houses. They were just alike, which I don't think would have mattered to him, but he was thrilled when they were installed. The fireplace in here is the same thing, salvaged from the farm that used to be where the mall is now."

"You mean Dickerson Mall?" She nodded. "I never saw the farm there, but I heard it was a big one. They raised pigs, didn't they?"

"Yes. Along with an assortment of other things. There are pictures of the old place out in the barn should you like to go through them. That's another thing my dad liked to collect was old pictures. He said they were a statement in time and that we wouldn't be able to go back and get them like you can now."

"I think I might have liked your father." She told Randal that everyone did. "Okay, let's see the rest of this place. And so you know, I think it's mighty tricky of you giving me this kind of history before I say yes or no."

"That's the plan."

They went through the rest of the house tougher. Chloe pointed out things that she remembered about the place, the things done to it, and even a few of the old pieces of furniture that she wanted to take out. Randal was nodding his consent even as he was telling her it wasn't a done deal. By the time they were going through the last room in the house, she knew he was going to take it.

They ended up back at their home. Randal and Scott had

loaded up the few pieces of furniture that she'd wanted. There were still a couple more...a cradle that had been her dads, some things that her mom had knitted before Chloe had been born. A couple of larger pieces would also make the move; the desk in the office, the chair that had been her grandda's, and the pipe collection that her dad had inherited from his grandda.

The trip through the house and shopping beforehand had been exhausting. Not just physically, but mentally too. When dinner was ready, she moved into the big room that Benton had completed only hours before, he told them, and saw that not only had Trent and Joe joined them, but so had Christina and TJ.

"I heard that you're going to get rid of your daddy's house. You know, at one time I had my eye on that place. I'm sure glad to know a fine man got it to live in." She thanked TJ and told him Randal was taking it. She was pleased when Randal didn't deny it. "Those women at that school will go nuts when they find out he's domesticated now. A homeowner with a job. They'll be all over him like turkey with dressing."

She was still laughing about the man's odd saying after everyone left. Chloe stood on the deck after the last of their taillights were gone and had a sudden thought. She wanted children. Looking up at Scott, she told him what she wanted, and he picked her up and swung her around. There would never be a dull moment with this man.

And Chloe was looking forward to the rest of her life laughing with and loving him.

~~~

Sterl wasn't sure about the piece of furniture he was looking at. It was nice, almost too nice to be as old as he'd been told. Walking around it a second time, he could see marks on it, some of them old, but they looked to him like they'd been put there on purpose. Like someone was trying to make the piece look distressed.

"Well, you gonna pay for it or stare it to death?" That was another thing he didn't like…how rude the little shit was that was selling it. "Like I said to you when you came in, I got three other people that want this particular piece. But I'm into a first come first serve kind of thing. And money talks."

"I don't think I want it." He felt better already after saying that. "It's a nice piece, but not really what I want for our home."

He and Noelle had decided that they'd get better deals if they didn't tell people they had a shop. Mostly it was to keep people from hitting on her and him, but it was working out for them so far. As he made his way to the door to leave, the kid called him back. Sterl turned but didn't go back to the area, and instead waited on the kid.

"You can't get a better deal than what I'm offering you, mister. You should really buy this piece off of me." Sterl felt his wolf stir along his skin. "I'm telling you right now, this is the real deal."

"I'm sure it is, but I'm not interested." He started walking backwards, keeping his eye on the kid. "I'm sure that those other people, one of them, will buy it off you."

"I don't think you understand." He nodded and knew he was close to the door now. His shadow was longer, what with the sun shining in from behind him. "I want you to come on back here and look at this piece again. You might decide that you like it."

Danger, his wolf seemed to scream at him. And when the kid pulled his shirt up and showed him the gun, Sterl knew that there was going to be bloodshed. His or the kid's, he wasn't sure, but he'd bet his last buck that Sterl might be the winner. He'd be hurt but he'd not be killed, like what was going to happen to the kid if he tried any shit with him.

"Look, I don't want the piece and I certainly don't want any trouble with you. I'm going to go away now, and you're going to stay where you are. I don't have time for your shit." Wrong tone and words, he knew that the moment that they left his mouth. "I'm sorry I can't give you what you want, but I don't want any trouble."

"You got yourself into trouble the moment you walked into the store when we weren't finished here." The word we had his wolf snarling at him. "You see, this is a robbery, and you went and fucked things up for us when we were about to pop us an old couple and take off with their goods. You're just about to be a statistic, buddy."

Sterl reached for Noelle and told her what was going on. Then he told her to call the police, but under no circumstances was she to come into the shop. He should have known that would get her dander up, as his dad was fond of saying.

I will not stay away. If you're hurt I won't sit around while it happens. Tell me why it is that you think you're any better at handling this situation by yourself than if I come in and help you. Is it because you think you're all special because you're a man and a Calhoun?

No. It's because if you come in I'm dead. She asked him why. *If you even so much as bump your toe against a piece of this furniture that is older than the two of us together, then Elijah is going to murder me. If you come in and I have to protect you from this idiot, then I'm going to die.*

Oh. A good answer, yes, but I still want to help you. The police are on their way. He thanked her. *Don't get hurt. I don't want you to get hurt or die, so please be careful.*

187

I promise you that I will. He told her what was going on. How the kid, whatever his name was, he was still trying to get him to follow him to the back of the store. *I think he's killed someone in here.*

Oh Sterl. I'm coming —

When he was hit from behind by the door, Sterl figured it was her. He nearly let his wolf go when he was tossed to the floor and shots were fired. Sterl thought for sure that they were both going to be hurt badly when the police came in with guns blazing.

Sterl was still sitting on the floor of the shop when his brother Trent spoke to him. If he'd said anything before that, Sterl wasn't sure. He was still trying to deal with the fact that he'd been shot and that the kid, a man really, was dead. The two people that the man had come there with, one his sister, the other his friend, were also dead.

"Are you all right?" He nodded and Trent told him to look at him. "Sterl, are you all right or do you need to go to the hospital?"

"I'm fine." He lifted his arm up to show him the bandage that had been put there when they declared it wasn't life-threatening. "It just scared the shit out of me is all. I was terrified that Noelle was going to get hurt."

"Yeah, I think Elijah was nearly ready to pick the dead man up and kill him again when he found out what had happened. They found the owners of the shop. They're both dead too." Sterl had already figured that out when he saw the body bags being taken out. "The police are thinking you were just in the wrong place at the wrong time."

"No shit." They both laughed a little, and Sterl finally felt like he could get up. Standing, he hugged Trent to him. "I have to tell you, I was scared out of my mind. Immortal or not, no one likes to be fired at."

"No. I wouldn't think so. Chloe is working with the men who are left in the department. She's really short staffed. Believe it or not, Dad and Grandda are volunteering to help her out by answering the phone and keeping an eye on the station while she gets things settled. She's not happy with me." Sterl asked him what he'd done now. "Why are you assuming this is my fault?"

"Because for whatever reason, you love aggravating the women of this family. I think you like being in the dog house with them." Trent grinned. "See? What did I tell you? What did you do to piss off Chloe?"

"She's going to be paid to work for the city." Sterl asked why that had pissed her off. "Because she's being paid by the pack to take care of the police department and the city. She's not happy with that. I told her that we have to pay her, it's part of the pack laws, and now she wants me to find them for her. I told her I'd look."

"I don't think there is a law." Trent only grinned. "Don't call me when she takes your head off. You're all on your own."

"I figured that it would make her mad at me just enough that she'd forget about all this other shit around her life." Sterl thought that might not help at all, but said nothing. "Anyway, if you're all right now, I'd like to get you home. Mom and Grandma want to pamper you a bit. I think Grandma thinks I'm lying to her about the extent of your injuries."

"She does. I've spoken to her and Mom." He had too, spending most of the time hearing his mom tell him how much she loved him and assuring her that he loved her as well. "Trent, do you think I'll spend the rest of my life with people trying to kill me? I mean, Christ, I've had a shitty life so far."

"You have, but it'll get better. Someday you'll meet your mate and she'll make it all worthwhile." Sterl wasn't so sure about that. "The good news is she won't be able to hurt you, so you can mark that off your list of scary shit."

"Thanks."

They made their way outside, where the truck that he and Noelle had been using was surrounded by yellow tape. Sterl didn't want to know why, but he thought he saw a plastic sheet over something near it.

When he crawled into bed just after midnight, he let his mind drift over the last several years. He'd been injured more than most, nearly killed more times than he wanted to think about. A she-devil after his seed, a demon that had to be killed, and then today. Sterl thought maybe he might find him a house on about a thousand acres and hide out there for the rest of his life. Grow a long beard, grow his own vegetables, and eat whatever came his way in the form of meat.

You'll do no such thing. Sterl sat up in bed and looked around. *I'm not there but I can feel your pain. What is it? Should I come there?*

Myra? She said of course it was her, who did he think it was. *Well, I have no idea. How the fuck can you feel me?*

I took a bit of you when we healed you. It's common to do that. Now, what is going on with your life, young pup? He asked her if she already knew. *Of course. But I should like to hear what you think about things. You're a survivor, young Sterling Calhoun, and I think that is what makes you so special to me.*

I don't want to be special to someone who can pop into my head whenever they want. She assured him that it wasn't like that. *Oh really? Then how did you know that I'd been in a funk?* Instead of answering him, as if he thought she would, she changed the subject.

Someone is coming your way soon. A person that, while I cannot see clearly, is coming all the same. He asked her if it was another devil or demon. *No, you've been promised that you are safe from both those monsters. No, this person will come to mean a great deal to your family. And to you.*

My mate. She said that she didn't think so. She thought it to be a male. *Okay, so this person is coming, and what am I supposed to do with him?*

I don't know that either. I'm only telling you what I've come to see. Sterl laid back down, sure now that he wasn't going to sleep. *Alta tells me that you've put on a little weight, and that your wolf is doing much better as well.*

She's wonderful, and I think you knew that when you sent her here. Myra only laughed. *I need to know something. Do you only dress the way you do for shock value, or do you actually enjoy looking like you do?*

I celebrate my life in color and design. You should try it sometime. She laughed again when he said nothing to her. *About this life that you're so ready to hide from...Sterl, you are much needed in this world. And to your family. They love you a great deal.*

Yes, they do. And I love them. But I'm sick of being beat to shit. He rolled to his back, still ready for the pain that was no longer there. *Maybe this man who comes here will want to run away with me as well.*

I should think you'd have to wait to see. Just as I will. He closed his eyes, knowing that he'd not sleep. *Rest, my young friend. You're going to need it.*

And just like that, Sterl felt himself fall to sleep.

Now Available in the Calhoun Men Series

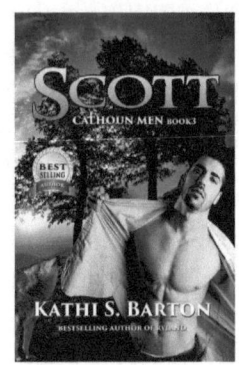

COMING SOON

Before You Go...

HELP AN AUTHOR

write a review

THANK YOU!

Share your voice and help guide other readers to these wonderful books. Even if it's only a line or two your reviews help readers discover the author's books so they can continue creating stories that you'll love. Login to your favorite retailer and leave a review. Thank you.

Kathi Barton, winner of the Pinnacle Book Achievement award as well as a best-selling author on Amazon and All Romance books, lives in Nashport, Ohio with her husband Paul. When not creating new worlds and romance, Kathi and her husband enjoy camping and going to auctions. She can also be seen at county fairs with her husband who is an artist and potter.

Her muse, a cross between Jimmy Stewart and Hugh Jackman, brings her stories to life for her readers in a way that has them coming back time and again for more. Her favorite genre is paranormal romance with a great deal of spice. You can visit Kathi on line and drop her an email if you'd like. She loves hearing from her fans. aaronskiss@gmail.com.

Follow Kathi on her blog: http://kathisbartonauthor. blogspot.com/